"You!" She Exclaimed, Finding Her Voice at Last.

"I can't believe it. You're the lowest man I've ever met."

And with that she attempted to walk past him out of the room. Calmly, imperturbably, he blocked her exit.

"You didn't think so last night, Jenna Martin," he drawled in a lowered voice, moving closer so that they were only a breath apart. To her dismay, she found herself longing for his arms to come around her. And then, without warning, his mouth was on hers.

SUZANNE CAREY

A reporter by training, a romance writer by choice, Suzanne likes to research her stories carefully and write about the places and people she knows best. For this reason, her books have a real-life quality that intrigues readers as much as it touches their hearts.

Dear Reader:

SILHOUETTE DESIRE is an exciting new line of contemporary romances from Silhouette Books. During the past year, many Silhouette readers have written in telling us what other types of stories they'd like to read from Silhouette, and we've kept these comments and suggestions in mind in developing SILHOUETTE DESIRE.

DESIREs feature all of the elements you like to see in a romance, plus a more sensual, provocative story. So if you want to experience all the excitement, passion and joy of falling in love, then SILHOUETTE DESIRE is for you.

I hope you enjoy this book and all the wonderful stories to come from SILHOUETTE DESIRE. I'd appreciate any thoughts you'd like to share with us on new SILHOUETTE DESIRE, and I invite you to write to us at the address below:

Karen Solem
Editor-in-Chief
Silhouette Books
P.O. Box 769
New York, N.Y. 10019

SUZANNE CAREY
Kiss and Tell

Silhouette Desire

Published by Silhouette Books New York

America's Publisher of Contemporary Romance

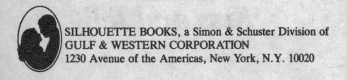
SILHOUETTE BOOKS, a Simon & Schuster Division of
GULF & WESTERN CORPORATION
1230 Avenue of the Americas, New York, N.Y. 10020

ISBN: 0-671-44822-6

First Silhouette Books printing June, 1982

10 9 8 7 6 5 4 3 2 1

Interior design by Joann Foster

America's Publisher of Contemporary Romance

Printed in the U.S.A.

Kiss and Tell

1

Jenna Martin stepped out of the cab into the sleet and slush of Chicago on a January afternoon. She waited, her teeth chattering as she huddled in her thin raincoat, while the porter loaded her luggage onto his cart.

As usual, O'Hare Airport traffic in the early dusk was a crush of cars and buses, a winking maze of taillights, and her cab had not been able to penetrate the inner ring of cars under the concrete portico. Icy rain crystals hit her stingingly in the face as she tipped the cabbie and turned to follow the porter across the clogged lanes of traffic toward the luminous lobby and ticket counter.

Ducking inside the double glass doors, she smoothed her windblown, honey-blond hair back into its braided chignon. At least it won't be sleeting in Florida, she thought, as she handed over her ticket to be marked and stapled with the luggage checks.

It was the most she could say for the assignment.

Four months ago both her parents and her brother Andy had been killed in a plane crash over the Atlantic as they returned from a European holiday. Now nothing much really mattered—not even the coveted Illinois Press Club award she'd received for her behind-the-scenes profile of a former Cook County state's attorney who had become governor. She wanted only to bury herself in trivia and safe routine. If the truth be told, she had wanted that even before her family tragedy.

Her life had seemed as gray as the Chicago winter skies since her father had transferred Paul Linski from

Second City magazine to the company's budding Tampa publication, *Bayside*, as its first managing editor.

No, to be precise, she thought, it had really started when she'd caught Paul and Rena Haas in the office that night just before he was to go. This discovery had been a particularly painful one because, less than a month earlier, she had finally pushed aside her misgivings and allowed Paul to become her lover. She had thought she wanted to marry him and believed he wanted the same thing. Even when Paul's lovemaking had turned out to be a bit impersonal and less memorable than the earth-shattering experience of her dreams, she had persisted in that attitude.

Mixed with the pain of rejection had been the awkwardness of seeing cool, bespectacled Paul pressing flushed Rena against a filing cabinet in the office storeroom with one of his hands under her skirt.

She would see Rena again now, for Rena had accompanied Paul to Tampa as one of his staff writers. And she would be working with Paul, at least part of the time, on the Tyrell assignment.

I hope the embarrassment has faded, she thought. I hope I can appear as cool and nonchalant as they are about what happened.

"Gate twenty-nine, 'B' Concourse," the airline agent was saying, as if for the second time. "Here's your ticket, miss."

He held out the magenta-and-white envelope.

Taking it, she turned, nearly colliding with a tall, striking man in a fleece-lined suede jacket. He was holding a Western hat. She had a fleeting impression of dark, straight hair, and eyes a most unusual shade of aquamarine.

"Oh . . . pardon me," she said a bit lamely, looking up at him from her five-foot-eight-inch height.

"Excuse *me*, ma'am." His voice, smooth and deep, held just a trace of Southern accent.

Incredibly, he was tanned a deep golden brown on that blustery January day. A Floridian, she thought, on his way home. She realized she was staring.

"Excuse me," she echoed. Clutching her carry-on luggage, she stepped around him and hurried away into the hive of the terminal to look for her gate.

She was a bare twenty minutes early. Only a few seats were still available, in the smoking section, and she selected a window seat as far forward as she could, resigning herself to smoke in her eyes.

Then, taking a place in the waiting area, Jenna sat quietly without opening the advance copy of the new *Second City* she'd brought from the office. Around her, children were whining or chasing each other about the passengers' feet. Young lovers about to part were whispering softly together. An old couple was sharing a newspaper. More than ever, she felt excruciatingly alone.

Outside sleet rattled against the thick terminal windows, a last reminder of winter. At the end of the accordian-pleated boarding tunnel the plane was being serviced.

Glancing back at the waiting area, she noted that the man with the Western hat and aquamarine eyes had arrived at the check-in counter. A moment later, he took a seat directly across the room. Jenna thought he raised one brow at her speculatively for a moment before unfolding his newspaper.

Andy crooked his brows a bit like that, she remembered, suddenly devastated. It was a habit he had acquired from their father. For a moment she was swimming in the pain of it again, back in the Lake Shore Drive apartment that was now hers alone, listening to news of the crash fall in leaden words from her Uncle Gene's mouth while her Aunt Sylvie stood by, helpless.

It was her Uncle Gene who had assumed his brother's place at the helm of CM Corporation, parent company of half a dozen thriving city magazines.

And it was Gene Martin who'd insisted she take on the Tyrell assignment, even if that meant she'd come face to face with Paul Linski again.

"I sent Ed Tyrell your piece about the 'guv' and he liked it well enough to let you do his story," her uncle had told her. "He's not an easy nut to crack and he doesn't give interviews, especially not in-depth personal ones. He's a man with a lot to tell and more to hide. But he said you seemed like a 'sensitive gal' and a 'pretty fine writer, for a woman.'"

Her hackles hadn't even stirred, as her uncle had probably intended them to.

"It's time for a piece on Tyrell that shows the man as he really is, and his eightieth birthday is the best news peg we're going to get. It's the kind of story you do best, one that will help build credibility for *Bayside.*"

Gene Martin had lit a cigar as he'd gazed out his window at the Tribune Tower across the way. "Anyway," he'd continued, "the change of scene'll do you good. It . . . might interest you to know that Rena approached Tyrell first about the story and got turned down flat."

Her head had come up at that, a glimmer of interest in her large hazel eyes.

"Said he didn't want to talk to any brash Yankee city-slicker intellectual," Gene Martin had added without expression.

Rena, she'd thought, seeing the skinny, curly-haired street kid who'd fought her way up from *City News.* A brash Yankee indeed. Someone Paul could take to bed without any commitment at all because she was "sophisticated and modern."

"You know you're special to me, Jen," Paul had said when they'd made their civilized good-byes. "But I'm a young man on the way up. There's room for a lot of women in my life. Rena doesn't mind that."

Standing there in her uncle's office, she'd pictured again his gray eyes, cold, behind the owlish glasses.

"I'll do it," she'd decided suddenly, almost surprising herself with the words.

Her Uncle Gene's arm had come around her. "You know, your daddy once interviewed Tyrell when he was a fresh-out-of-school reporter on the Tallahassee *Democrat,*" he'd said softly. "The old man remembers him."

Now, sitting in the air terminal about to embark on the assignment, she wasn't sure she'd made a wise choice. The tragedy, she felt, had left her too burnt out to write. And Ed T. Tyrell, as he neared eighty, was a complex and difficult man, one who would require all her skill to interview, despite any good memories he might have of her father.

Oh, Tyrell was quotable, she knew—*if* he would let you quote him. A dazzling manipulator in his prime, he could tell you inside out and firsthand about every important political deal cut in Florida during the past forty-five years—*if* he would tell the truth.

A three-term Florida legislator, he had once been speaker of the house. Then he had retired from public politics at the age of forty-seven to be the maker of governors and senators instead. Still vigorous for his age, he remained a figure to reckon with in state politics, a latent power in banking circles, and the patriarch of his family and its far-flung business interests.

But Ed T., as his friends called him, and his wily complexity weren't the only problems. His family, her uncle had admitted, was opposed to the article.

There was a twenty-nine-year-old grandson, Edward Yancey Tyrell, called Neddy, a playboy without much business sense, who might be a possible source. And there was a seventy-six-year-old, probably somewhat dotty Aunt Bliss, who could and perhaps would offer some stories.

But the rest of the family, she knew, would be suspicious, protective, and closemouthed. Foremost among them would be Ed T.'s only living son and right-hand

11

man, Duke. At thirty-four, he was a heartbreaker with women, by all accounts, and a hard-as-nails business-man-rancher.

In all but title now he was the man who oversaw the family's citrus and cattle interests. Of all the Tyrells, her uncle had said, Duke was the most dead set against the story project, expressing concern that his father might be exposed to gossip on the eve of his eightieth birthday.

"Young Tyrell is a powerful man," her uncle had warned. "He usually gets his way."

Jenna's chin jutted out a little. For as long as it took to complete the assignment, she would stay on the job, despite Duke Tyrell's opposition. If there was a story to be gotten, she would get it. I may lack Rena's brashness and street-kid savvy, she thought, but I have enough determination for both of us.

She started as the airline agent began calling the passengers to the gate, then gathered up her newspaper, makeup case, and Polish leather camera bag.

To her surprise, the man with the aquamarine eyes halted beside her as she settled into her seat.

From her sitting position he seemed even taller than before—six-feet, four-inches at least—as he towered above her in his smoky brown suede jacket and superbly tailored dark brown slacks that seemed sculpted to the curves of his thigh muscles.

He was glancing at his ticket, clearly puzzled, and then at the seat numbers displayed overhead. Finally his eyes met hers.

"Pardon me," he said politely in that deep voice of his with its lazy vowels and faintly softened consonants, "but I think you may have taken my seat."

Jenna stared. On closer inspection she found him to be quite the most good-looking man she'd ever seen. Dark brows drew together over those arresting eyes with their fringe of thick lashes in a way that suggested he could master any situation the moment he had figured it out. His lean, tanned face with its beginnings of squint and frown lines and its strongly modeled features just missed being handsome in a classical sense. Yet somehow that faintly rough-hewn quality made him all the more interesting and attractive. His jaw spoke of a self-confidence that could become wrongheaded and stubborn at its extreme, his mouth of a passionate nature, though it hinted, too, at humor and a rare, fleeting tenderness.

Stop that, she thought, pulling herself up sharply. He's going to think you're some kind of idiot. This is the kind of behavior that will put you at a distinct disadvantage when you meet Duke Tyrell.

In fact, she thought, continuing to stare, this man could *be* Tyrell. Except for that tenderness I sense, he fits the description perfectly. But of course that was impossible.

"I . . . deliberately chose a seat by the window," she managed at last. "I'm afraid you must be mistaken."

The man's frown deepened slightly. "I don't *think* so," he said, leaning down to show her his ticket.

Jenna dug in her purse and extracted her own to compare. "Yours is thirty-four A, for aisle," she explained after a moment. "Mine is thirty-four W, the window seat. Elementary alphabet. Sorry."

He shrugged, the brows smoothing a bit. "Well," he said, "so am I—for troubling you and because this is my first flight out of Chicago."

Immediately she felt a stab of regret, wished she'd been wrong and that she could take back her rather superior remark. Probably he seldom traveled outside his own bailiwick.

"That's okay," she said, watching with an interest she couldn't suppress as he removed the suede jacket and stowed it overhead to reveal well-built shoulders and chest in a cream-colored string-knit sweater.

He sat beside her, completely filling up the space with his tall frame, unable to stretch out his long legs very much.

"In fact," she added, "you may *have* the window seat if you don't mind leaving my things stashed as they are."

I've flown out of here more times than I can count. But I don't think you're going to see much in this weather.

He glanced at her in surprise. "Why, thank you, I'd really appreciate it."

They made the transfer in the narrow space, brushing up against each other in the process. Jenna caught the alluring aroma of tobacco blended with a mossy after-shave.

For a purely sensual moment, she wondered what it would be like to be kissed by this enticing stranger, held fast in those powerful-looking arms. I'll bet making love to him would be about as earth-shattering as I could stand, she thought.

Giving him a faintly embarrassed smile, as if she thought he could read her mind, she sat down again and retreated into her magazine. Without really seeing anything, she gazed blindly at the way photos and layout and stories in this latest issue worked together.

There was no denying that her seatmate for this trip overflowed with animal magnetism, even if she weren't in the market, just now, for a new beau. But it's likely he isn't very sophisticated, she thought. Paul could probably talk circles around him. I imagine he's interested only in cattle and hunting and country music. Probably he drives a pickup truck with a shotgun mounted in the rear window.

A few minutes later the seat belt warning sign came on and a stewardess came by to ask that their seats be locked in the upright position. Then they were pulling away from the terminal and out along a broad runway winking with blue lights in the early, sleeting dusk, gathering speed and lifting off into the air.

They had only a brief glimpse of the city lights in the vicinity of the airport before thick gray clouds enveloped them. Turning from the window, her temporary companion looked at her.

"You were right," he said. "I shouldn't have put you to

the trouble of switching seats. At the very least, let me buy you a drink in return."

"I'm not much for alcohol," said Jenna, but when the stewardess came around she allowed the tall Southerner to order her a vodka Collins, a mild drink that could be sipped indefinitely and would weaken a bit as the ice cubes melted.

His own choice was Scotch on the rocks. Their hands touched as they reached simultaneously for their glasses on the stewardess's plastic tray and she felt an inescapable little thrill from the contact. She noted the way his nails, blunt and carefully manicured, were white against his tanned skin. He wore no wedding ring.

"Cheers," he said, saluting her with one brow crooked in the way she'd noticed before, his eyes for the moment curiously flat and appraising. "I hope you enjoy your vacation."

"Thanks," said Jenna. "But this is a working trip. I'm a writer on assignment for my magazine. Or a lamb on the way to the slaughter, depending on how you look at it."

His brow shot up even further.

"It's a . . . particularly difficult assignment," she said. "I expect to have to deal with some people who don't want to talk to me at all."

"Oh, I see." He sipped his Scotch, still regarding her in that appraising way.

"I suppose we should introduce ourselves," she added after a moment. "I'm Jenna Martin and I work for *Second City* magazine." She nodded at the issue that lay open in her lap.

"Tom . . . Courtenay." She noticed and wondered at his slight hesitation, even as he took her hand in his for a brief, warm handclasp.

"How do you do?" she said. "I . . . don't mean to imply that I'm really such a lamb. I may be young and less experienced than some, but I'm tenacious as the very devil if I have to be."

Something flickered in his aquamarine eyes, a certain momentary satisfaction. It's as if the battle is joined, she thought with a little jolt of surprise. But why should he . . .

"You didn't say what you did for a living," she reminded him.

"Oh." He shrugged. "I have a small ranch near Brooksville, in Florida. And this trip wasn't a vacation for me either." He didn't elaborate.

Surprisingly, after they shared dinner and a desultory conversation, she managed to sleep a little, stirring only at the pinging of the cabin bell. She awoke to hear the stewardess's voice coming over the loudspeaker again, asking the passengers to rebuckle their seat belts in preparation for landing.

She was embarrassed to discover that her head had slipped off her pillow onto Tom Courtenay's broad shoulder. Momentarily, she caught again the aroma of tobacco and mossy after-shave, mingled this time with the warm, intimate skin scent of his neck.

Quickly, she sat up, buckled on her belt.

"Please forgive me," she began, all too aware of the flush that had spread on her cheeks and the amusement in his aquamarine eyes. "It was the drink. I usually don't sleep so soundly on a plane, and *never* on a stranger's shoulder."

His mouth curved into a smile and he laid one warm hand lightly and briefly over hers, where they rested in her lap.

"Don't apologize," he said. "I liked it. And I didn't think you were being forward."

He turned to look out the window. Her ears were popping from their descent and she yawned several times to ease the discomfort.

"We're coming in over the beaches," Tom Courtenay said after a moment. "I can see the lights now. And the sky's clear, with a bright moon. It's a lovely night."

She leaned behind him to peer out the window and thus they were a breath apart as he turned back toward her.

"There's room for us both to watch," he said with another flicker of amusement, putting one arm lightly around her. She would have felt like a prude if she'd pulled away.

As they gazed through the rounded double-glass pane, their plane began to circle over Tampa Bay and she could see, stretched out across the black water, the strings of lights he said were the Gandy and Howard Frankland bridges.

"Beautiful," she said. "They're like necklaces on velvet."

Then they were coming in low over a shopping mall and a multilane interstate to touch down on a broad runway. She could see the silhouettes of palm trees.

"Home," said Tom Courtenay with a satisfied little sigh.

After taxiing smoothly down the runway, they drew up at the gate. Politely, her new acquaintance helped her on with her coat, then slung his own jacket across his shoulders.

"People think we're in the tropics here," he remarked. "But we've been having a cold winter."

Yet in the tunnel that connected the plane to the gate she felt the warm, moist, incredibly soft rush of tropical air. Not cold the way *I* mean it, she thought.

With the tall rancher still beside her she stepped onto one of the "people-mover" trams that transferred passengers to the airport's main terminal. She rode just ahead of him down the two-story escalator to the baggage-claim area, obviously pleasing him with her praise of a huge hanging copper sculpture of airborne pelicans.

As she stood waiting by the baggage carousel, he was still at her side, standing close in the crush of people.

17

Several times he brushed against her and each time she felt the same unbidden thrill at the contact, remembered his casual arm about her. Almost regretfully she realized that in a moment their bags would emerge and then he'd probably be offering his hand, wishing her a pleasant stay and saying good-bye.

A man as gorgeous as that must have somebody to come home to, she argued, even if he isn't wearing a wedding ring. She thought again that, though he might be no intellectual, he'd be a warm and demanding lover, not someone to take no for an answer the way Paul repeatedly had done before finally winning her submission.

Thoughtfully, she bit her lip. Maybe that's what I need, she thought—someone like Tom Courtenay, who really isn't even my type, to make me stop thinking about Paul, ease the pain of losing Mom and Dad and Andy. But casual love affairs were against her principles and she wondered if she'd really take the opportunity if it were offered.

Almost absently, she lifted her two bags off the carousel. Beside her, Tom Courtenay was saying something.

She turned, expecting to hear a polite good-bye, and saw that there was anything but good-bye in his light, beautiful eyes.

"Someone meeting you?" he asked.

"No." She stood a bit awkwardly, gazing up at him, her head coming only to his shoulder.

"I don't have to see my editor until tomorrow," she said. "I have reservations at a place called the International Inn and I thought I'd pick up my rental car, just go on over . . ."

"It's much too early for that," said Tom Courtenay firmly, using that masterful tone she'd known him to be capable of. "I'd consider it a favor if you'd keep me company for a steak. That wasn't much of a supper we had."

He was asking her—or maybe telling her—to go out with him.

"I . . . don't know if I should," she began, then realized how foolish she sounded. "I mean, I should pick up my rental car . . ." And then she was kicking herself because she seemed to be turning him down.

He wasn't the sort to let her. "We can arrange to have the company drop it off for you in the morning," he said, picking up her heaviest bag. "C'mon—my car's here at the airport."

The matter completely out of her hands, she followed him to the rental car desk, where he effortlessly made the necessary arrangements. Then they were riding up in an elevator to the parking garage.

As they stepped outside, the full difference in temperature and humidity between Chicago and Tampa hit Jenna, and she exclaimed, "It's wonderful—almost seductive. So warm. I feel like my skin could drink the air!"

His eyes glittered at her. "Beautifully put," he said. "You really must be a writer."

She was forced to eat her speculation that Tom Courtenay drove a pickup truck as he fitted his key into the door lock of a cream Mercedes convertible with toast-colored top and leather upholstery.

The door closed after her with a rich, heavy *chunk*. I wonder how big his "small ranch near Brooksville" is, she thought. I have the sudden feeling he's a very wealthy man.

Tossing his jacket in the back seat, he got in beside her, switched on the ignition, and lowered the windows to admit the air. Then he turned quietly to look at her, seeming in that moment to loom unexpectedly close.

"You have a very tender-looking mouth, Jenna Martin," he said, his voice taking on a husky note. "I've been wanting to do something to it ever since we sat down together on the plane. And I *would* have, if I hadn't thought you'd ring for the stewardess."

Before she could reply, his arms came around her, as strong and demanding as she'd thought they'd be. His mouth, at once rough and tender, had taken complete possession of hers in a kiss like no other she'd ever known.

Surprisingly, she felt no fear. Though he was a stranger, and they were alone in his car in a parking garage half a continent from familiar territory, she found her arms slipping around to cradle the warm, hard muscles of his back, her lips parting to accommodate his tongue's sweet invasion.

The little gesture of surrender was like a goad. He held her even more tightly, one hand moving down to cradle the seat of her caramel-colored wool cashmere pants and pull her up against him. Lean and tactile, the capable fingers that had so drawn her eye on the plane were pressing into her through the soft fabric, cupping her firm, tender curves.

In her nostrils, the scent of him was like a powerful aphrodisiac. Desire—frank and sensual and aching— surged through her in a way she'd only read about before. Unbidden, her lips communicated it to him and his kiss deepened, taking complete possession of her mouth. His tongue, so strenuous and rough and tender, seemed to seek out her deepest recesses and make them his.

Finally he drew back, his breath on her warm and intimate for the space of several seconds, and then he kissed her again, gently this time, teasing at the corners of her mouth.

"Just as tender as I thought," he remarked, his eyes gleaming at her soft confusion.

For a moment Jenna could not speak, unable to retreat as easily as he from their powerful contact. Then: "What must you think of me?" she whispered.

He smoothed a strand of her hair into place, settled her back against her seat, and shifted into reverse before answering.

"That you're a desirable—and desiring—woman," he said in that deep, soft, Southern voice of his. "But I'd already guessed as much."

2

Before she could change her mind about going out with him, he had backed out of the parking space and maneuvered the beautiful car with its deeply purring engine down the curving exit ramp to pay an exorbitant parking fee.

"You should have used the long-term lot, sir," the attendant chided him.

He nodded. "I was in a hurry."

The gate went up and he stepped on the accelerator. They shot forward onto a multilane highway, moving smoothly into a lane marked KENNEDY BOULEVARD.

"There's your motel," he said, making a left at the first light.

Jenna turned to gaze after it. "Maybe I shouldn't have come," she said, hating her own prim-sounding words. "I hardly know you."

Tom Courtenay gave her a swift, hard glance as if he didn't quite believe her protestation was sincere. Then he reached over to pat her hand.

"No," he said. "You were right to trust me. I'll only go as far as you let me, Jenna Martin." It wasn't exactly a promise that eased her mind.

The restaurant he'd chosen, Bern's Steak House, was another hint that he was no poor, small-time rancher. There's only one word for this place and that's *opulent,* Jenna thought, as she walked beside her impromptu date into a two-story-high lobby with an elegant curving staircase.

She smoothed her caramel slacks and sweater. "Are you sure I'm dressed all right?"

"A beautiful woman is dressed right for Bern's whatever she's wearing," he said gallantly.

Deferentially, with almost European courtesy, the headwaiter showed them to an intimate, secluded table. With a smoothness born of familiarity and practice, her companion ordered their wine and steaks, choosing a queen filet for her smaller appetite.

"All right," he said, leaning back to take her hand as the waiter hurried away. "We need to remedy this 'strangers' business. You first. I want to hear everything. You needn't start at the beginning. Five years of age will do."

At first, she tried to shrug off his interest. But as the wine arrived, and then their steaks, she found herself opening up to this masterful stranger, telling him things she'd never shared before, even with Paul—how she'd been punished for putting pepper in another girl's milk at the North Shore Country Day School, about the dog she'd lost when she was eleven, the way she wanted to write novels someday.

The things she loved best, and missed most, about her parents and Andy came inevitably to the fore. But the telling didn't seem so maudlin, now. It was more like a natural sharing of her experience with another human being.

He was a good listener, interjecting a question or comment when it was called for, attentive as he demolished his huge T-bone and lit his pipe afterward.

"Men friends?" he asked at one point, arching one dark brow at her.

"Some," she admitted. "Nobody special right now. Seems to me it's your turn to do the talking."

"You're right." Unobtrusively, he picked up the check, laying several large bills on the tray. "We can do that at your place," he said, rising to pull out her chair.

"My . . . place?" She gave him a quick glance and

realized she was not expected to impede their smooth exit.

"Sure," said Tom Courtenay in her ear with just a hint of laughter. "They have a nice little bar with a dance floor . . ."

At her motel he stood by while she registered, then tipped a bellhop to take her things upstairs. Once again, she thought, my affairs have been effortlessly managed.

The bar was small and dark, with only a pocket-sized area set aside for dancing. There wasn't much of a crowd taking advantage of the music provided by a handful of country-and-western musicians.

Well, she'd guessed his taste in music correctly, at least. But far from putting him down for it, she rather liked the homespun, all-American image his enjoyment of country music gave him. Surprisingly, that image didn't conflict with his air of mastery or in any way diffuse the vibrant animal magnetism he possessed.

Tom Courtenay is the most virile man I've ever met, she admitted to herself, her every fiber aware of his tall presence as he walked in beside her. It won't surprise me if I have to fend him off at my door tonight.

At the moment he seemed to want nothing more than drinks and conversation and the chance to hold her in his arms on the dance floor. But she couldn't forget the way it had been between them in his car at the airport parking garage, the way he seemed able to provoke her into throwing caution to the winds and doing what he wanted.

No, she thought. I don't imagine he'll be satisfied with drinks and dancing for long. When he makes his move, I'm not sure how I'll handle it.

They settled at their table. Without consulting her, he ordered drinks, the same ones he'd asked for on the plane.

Then he sat smiling at her with unmistakable admiration in his eyes. Yet he seemed a trifle uncomfortable, too, she thought suddenly—as if he knew a secret that ought to be shared, one he wasn't ready to part with yet.

She smiled back uncertainly, wondering if he would tell her anything about himself.

At that moment the combo finished a fast number and took up a slow and sentimental melody. One of the guitarists, a man with graying fair hair and a weathered face, began to sing in a deep soft voice.

"Shall we?" asked Tom Courtenay, taking her hand.

Going into his arms on the little dance floor, Jenna found that the tall rancher could move to music as well as he could kiss. Despite his height, he was lithe and graceful, as powerful as a panther and as economical of motion.

With a sigh, she relaxed into his lead. Paul hadn't been much of a dancer—willing to perform only a few disco steps when it had been the "in" thing to do. Her few dates since Paul's departure, mostly with Robert Czerny, a Northwestern University music professor, hadn't included any dancing and she'd missed the pleasure she always found in it.

Involuntarily, she moved closer in Tom Courtenay's embrace and he responded by drawing her nearer still, putting both arms around her. She could feel his steady heartbeat through the string-knit sweater. The warmth of his body radiated the same vibrant sexuality that had already so disarmed her.

Again one hand strayed to her hip, testing her movement and inviting her to intimate knowledge of his hard-muscled thighs.

Here on the dance floor they were matched length for length, despite his greater height, and she was suddenly conscious of his desire for her.

Heedless of the consequences for the moment, she pressed herself to him, her lips parting with pleasure at the blunt, passionate way he was nuzzling her neck.

We might as well be in bed together, the way I can feel him, she thought.

The song ended on a minor key.

"Know what, Jenna Martin?" asked her partner, just

perceptibly tightening his arms before he slackened them to loosely hold her hands. "You're awfully good to hold."

She looked into his aquamarine eyes. "You're not so bad yourself," she said, liking the way her hands felt, resting in his.

By tacit agreement, they spent most of the next forty-five minutes on the dance floor, lost in the blurring sensations of touch and scent and movement and the plaintive, desire-filled lyrics of country-and-western love songs.

Finally he glanced at his watch, expensively thin and gleaming against his wrist, and led her quietly over to the bar to pay the tab.

"I still have to drive out to Brooksville tonight," he explained, then paused. "Unless you invite me to stay here with you."

She flushed and prayed he wouldn't notice. But they had stepped out of the bar into the moderately bright lobby.

"What time *is* it?" she asked, keeping her voice under control.

"Nearly eleven thirty."

Before she could come up with an alternate suggestion, he was pressing the elevator button and stepping in beside her. With a smooth hiss, the elevator door shut and they were alone. He took her into his arms.

"Well?" he asked, the words punctuated by soft little kisses. "Are you going to let me stay?"

He was, after all, a stranger. "No . . . I couldn't . . ." she began.

Her denial was smothered by another kiss just as the door slid open on the third floor to reveal two teenaged boys with an ice bucket.

She drew back, embarrassed, as they exchanged places with the teens and she dug in her purse for the motel room key with lowered eyes. Her room was only a few steps away, just around the corner. Nervously she fitted the key into the lock and partially opened the door.

"I'm afraid this will have to be good night," she whispered. "I'm . . . not the sort of girl to do what you suggest . . ."

"Not *girl*," said Tom Courtenay, easing those strong arms about her again, though he made no attempt to step beyond the door. "I'd say *woman*. Why send me away? I really do want to sleep with you and I guarantee I'll give satisfaction . . ."

Jenna's cheeks burned at his frankness. No one had talked to her quite so matter-of-factly or openly before, and for a moment she thought she would slap his face. But something stayed her hand.

"Please," she begged softly. "Don't spoil . . ."

Something flickered in his eyes. "All right," he said, his voice as steady as if they'd been discussing the price of beef cattle. "I remember promising I'd go only as far as you let me. Good night." And with a faint brushing of his mouth against hers, he was gone.

Quickly, she stepped inside and shut the door, slipping the chain into place, not so much for safety's sake as to prevent him from returning to see how she was shaking. Tears of frustration were tracing her cheeks.

The fact is, I *wanted* him to stay, she admitted, hugging herself. And now I probably won't see him again.

It was a long time before she fell asleep.

A knock on her motel room door awoke her. After finally drifting off, she had slept, as usual, like a stone and she woke disoriented, grasping after barely remembered snatches of dreams. Filtering in around the heavy window drapes, the billion-watt Florida sunlight told her it was morning.

Discreetly, the knock came again, and her previous night's adventure flooded back to her. Was he at her door?

"Who is it?" she called in a voice that quavered a little in spite of her attempt at control.

"Bellboy," came the response. "I have something for you, miss."

Tom Courtenay's little joke? Was he waiting on the other side of the door to throw his arms around her?

Quickly she pulled her robe about her and unfastened the chain. To her surprise it *was* the bellboy. He was holding out a florist's box.

"These just came for you, miss," he said, lounging a bit in the doorway to remind her of a tip.

Her duty to the bellhop done, she closed the door and sat down on the unused bed to open the silvery cardboard box. Nested inside, in waxy green florist's paper, was a nosegay of gardenias—incredibly creamy and sweet-smelling against their glossy dark leaves. There was also a card. *"Thanks for a pleasant evening,"* it proclaimed in a scrawling masculine hand. There was no signature.

Thrilled at the tribute but dashed by his terse little note, she buried her nose in the fragrant petals. Surely he'll call, she thought, if only to try again. She couldn't picture an apology.

But she was forced to give up even that hope when an hour after her rental car had been delivered and two hours after she'd received the flowers there had still been no call. If she waited much longer, she'd be late for lunch with Paul and later still in arriving at the Tyrell homestead.

On impulse she picked up the phone and dialed the Brooksville operator, asked for Tom Courtenay's number. The least I can do, she thought, is thank him in return.

But after a thorough search the operator confessed she could find no such listing. Jenna's heart sank. Unlisted phone number, she thought. Or phony name. Probably that's it—he's a married man. They don't all wear wedding bands.

Thoroughly shaken and disillusioned but perversely treasuring her gardenias, she checked out. That's that, she told herself firmly as she located Habana Avenue on the map of Tampa she'd spread beside her on the seat. I won't see him again.

Bayside's Habana Avenue offices, she discovered, were situated in a renovated cigar factory. Its ancient bricks had been sandblasted to a rosy clean hue. The antique wooden double doors opened to reveal a high-ceilinged lobby with bare brick walls that were studded sparsely with abstract art.

A brunette secretary greeted her.

"Mr. Linski is expecting you," she said, beckoning Jenna to follow her back through the maze of cubicles where writers and layout artists worked.

There was no way to avoid stopping by Rena Haas' desk to say hello.

"You're looking good, Jenna," said her former rival, as ingratiatingly self-confident as ever as she appraised Jenna's oyster-beige raw-silk suit, her emerald-colored silk shantung blouse, and her gold jewelry. "I was awfully sorry to hear about your folks," Rena added.

"Thank you." She didn't know what else to say. Rena would probably have no more sense than to show up at the Tyrells' in a denim skirt, she thought.

"I hope you enjoy doing *my* story," her former rival was saying, as usual making no bones about any jealousy she might feel. Her green eyes narrowed at Jenna. "Wish *I* were the one invited to stay at the Tyrells' ranch with Duke Tyrell in arm's reach. . . ."

Hearing their voices, Paul had stepped out of his private office.

"Jenna!" he exclaimed, coming forward to put both arms around her. There was an enthusiasm in his voice she hadn't heard for a while. "It's really good to see you," he added, standing back to look at her. "You seem exactly the same. *Are* you?"

"Not quite." To her surprise, Jenna realized that her first thought at his remark had been of Tom Courtenay's kiss, not of the intimacy she and Paul had once shared.

"Poor lamb," said Paul, who'd come north for the funeral. "Of course not. You've been through so much." He started to draw her away, toward his office. "I've made our lunch reservations at Rough Riders," he said, adding with his passion for facts, "Teddy Roosevelt trained his men here for the assault on San Juan Hill, so he's part of the local history. The restaurant that's named for him is in another cigar factory over in Ybor City, much larger than ours, with whole suites of shops and offices."

"Am I invited too?" Rena called brightly after them. She'd been unable to keep a hint of possessiveness out of her voice. "I have to have lunch somewhere."

"Sorry, Rena. Not today." The quick backward glance Paul gave Rena from behind his thick spectacles was at least as cold as any *she'd* known, Jenna thought. So Rena was wearing a bit thin with him already.

Without further comment, Paul ushered her into his office and shut the door. She stood for a moment looking at him, wondering what she'd found so irresistible about his slight build and faintly stooped shoulders, the sandy hair that would thin early, those cold, calculating eyes.

His blessed intellect, she thought. I was impressed. And he *is* a good journalist. He'll make an even better editor with that hard-edged personality of his.

Then, when no words had been exchanged for a moment and it seemed he might put an arm about her again, she quickly took a seat in one of the sculptured Kelly-green chairs and looked around at the artwork. Some she recognized. She'd been at his side when he'd purchased it in the little galleries that lined Chicago's Oak Street. But there were some new prints, lovely things.

"Rauschenberg," he supplied. "Jim Dine. From the graphics studio of the university here."

She nodded. "Tell me about the Tyrells," she said, effectively forestalling any personal remark. "Rena said something about staying at the ranch."

He shrugged, lit a cigarette.

"That's right," he said. "I can't figure the old man out—first he won't do the story at all and then he insists on taking you to his bosom." He paused. "It won't be all sweetness and light, though. He's a wily old cuss and his son is adamantly opposed to having you in the house."

She nodded again. "Uncle Gene told me."

"Well . . . so long as you're warned." Shifting a little in his chair, he opened a desk drawer and withdrew a folder.

"Here's a file on the family—everything we could dig up in three weeks plus some preliminary notes Rena made. Whatever you think of her, she's a good researcher."

"I agree." Calmly she accepted the folder but did not open it. "Rena's all right."

He gave her a look. "Why don't you glance through those things over lunch?" he suggested, getting to his feet again. "We can talk about the Tyrells . . . old times . . ."

"I'd rather skip the old times, if you don't mind," she said shortly, rising also, then added as sweetly as she could, "I'm sure you understand, Paul, so soon after Mom and Dad . . ."

Instantly he was solicitous, correct. "Of course I do," he said. "It's just that I've missed you—a lot."

It was quite an admission, she knew, for him to make. What did you expect, she asked him silently, but a casual attitude? Did you think I would carefully tend the flame?

"Maybe after you finish the story . . ." he added, leaving the sentence hanging in midair.

"Maybe." With a faint smile, she opened the door to the outer office. It would be easier to work with Paul, she guessed, if she kept him at a distance but didn't push him away altogether.

As it turned out, when they were finally seated across from each other at Rough Riders, a small, intimate restaurant tucked away in the old cigar factory complex, they talked neither of the Tyrells nor of old times. Jenna had left the Tyrell folder on the seat of the car, and anyway, Paul was happy enough during lunch to tell her of the magazine he'd helped bring to life, his plans and hopes for its future.

Then, without even lighting a second cigarette, he was paying their bill and driving her back, dropping her off beside her rented car at her request.

For a moment she stood in the gravel parking lot after he'd gone in, just soaking up the early afternoon sunlight, so powerful and brilliant after Chicago in midwinter, noticing the way it traced the live oaks' precise little leaves.

Then she glanced at her watch. It was one twenty already. She would only make her appointment with the Tyrells if she left immediately.

Following the directions she'd been given, she located the nearest I-75 entrance ramp and headed north. In a surprisingly short time she had left behind Tampa's few modest skyscrapers, its tree-shaded streets of wooden bungalows and concrete-block ranches. She emerged in a rolling countryside of pine scrub and oak pasture dotted with cattle and orange groves. An occasional flat, swampy stretch was marked by clusters of bald cypresses, gray-brown now with winter.

Too bad I didn't have time to go through that folder before meeting the terrible Tyrells, she thought. But it wouldn't do to get off on the wrong foot by arriving late.

And then her thoughts returned, unbidden, to Tom Courtenay, and she spent some time seeking a reasonable explanation for his behavior.

Roughly an hour had elapsed by the time she reached the San Antonio–St. Lee turnoff. Just before reaching the hamlet of San Antonio, she turned again, back north, on a narrow county highway marked TYRELL ROAD. It wasn't long before she had arrived at the entrance to the Tyrell property, a cypress gate marked BAR-T.

Huge, venerable oaks hung with swaying Spanish moss bordered the gravel drive. She had expected an antebellum red brick mansion with white pillars and graceful Corinthian capitals, the traditional Southern symbol of wealth and power. But the Tyrell house wasn't like that. Rounding a bend in the drive, she saw it—a large, rambling mid-Victorian structure built, like the gate, of weathered cypress. It was a house that had casually and repeatedly been added to and embellished over the years. Broad verandas and shuttered windows provided cooling shade that would be quite welcome, she thought, in the blazing summers.

She noted tennis courts, and a swimming pool situated where bathers would have an unobstructed view of the gently rising citrus-planted ridges that stretched to the horizon. A covered walkway connected the main house to a multiple-car garage. Set apart and partially screened by several rows of trees were the barns and stables and other outbuildings, a collection of small dwellings that must house the hired help.

Unconsciously, Jenna relaxed the pressure of her foot on the accelerator, prolonging the moment of her approach as long as possible. To her, this rambling, unassuming seat of the Tyrell clan spelled power in a way that the typical Southern manse could not have done.

Far from being brazen, that power would be hidden under an affable and charming exterior. I'll have to tread carefully, she thought.

Even as she gave herself that final warning, she pulled up at the steps to the main house's broad veranda. A tall, weathered man in blue jeans and checked shirt stepped down to greet her, as promptly as if he'd been waiting all afternoon.

"Hi," he said. "I'm Wayne Keeper, Mister Duke's right-hand man. Y'all must be Miss Martin."

"Yes," she said, smoothing her skirt as she got out. "Hello."

He nodded. "Mister Ed T. is expecting you," he said. "If you'll give me your keys, I'll send a boy to park the car and fetch your things."

She complied. With one hand just touching her elbow, Wayne Keeper drew her into a flagstone, portrait-lined foyer and quickly down a central hall to a large, thickly carpeted study that overlooked the rear lawns.

"Miss Jenna Martin," her escort announced, leaving her.

Behind the enormous carved desk that looked as if it had come from a European castle sat the man she had come to meet.

At nearly eighty, he seemed as vigorous as she'd expected, though his white hair had thinned and his skin was mottled, his muscles slack now on the once-powerful frame. Large, bony hands rested with latent authority on the desk in front of him. Brown eyes regarded her intently from behind gold-rimmed spectacles.

"Good afternoon, Mr. Tyrell," she said, approaching with what she hoped was calm confidence and holding out her hand.

He took it and held it warmly.

"How do you do, young lady?" he said in a deep voice, with cadences that were somehow familiar. "Glad you could come. May I call you Jenna, sweetheart? You've probably heard that I knew your daddy."

"I'd like that fine," she murmured, her hand still in his even as she became aware of another presence in the room. A tall, dark man in blue jeans and a blue work shirt stood beside the window, his face turned discourteously away from her. Something about that posture, the set of those broad shoulders, gave her disturbing pause.

Ed T.'s brown eyes, so bright and yet opaque, had followed her gaze. "I'd like you to meet my son Duke," he said. "Duke, say hello to Jenna Martin."

With a scarcely defined gesture that seemed to hint at reluctance, Duke Tyrell turned to face her, and she found herself staring with astonishment and rapidly mounting fury into Tom Courtenay's aquamarine eyes.

3

He didn't move nearer or hold out his hand.

"You!" she exclaimed, finding her voice at last, though she was quivering with anger. "It's monstrous! I can't believe anyone would sink so low."

With a faint quirk of one dark brow, Duke Tyrell saluted her. Only later, in retrospect, would she separate the discomfort and faint pangs of guilt he displayed from his arrogance.

"Thomas Courtenay Tyrell, at your service," he said. "Provided, of course, that you don't make unreasonable demands."

She could think of nothing to reply without resorting to unbecoming language, so she glared at him in helpless fury.

"I take it you've already met my son," said the old man to Jenna, his matter-of-fact remark breaking the emotionally charged silence. "What have you been doing to this pretty young lady, Duke, to make her so mad at you?"

"Misrepresenting himself, among other things," she replied in a stony voice when Duke chose not to respond. "We were . . . seatmates on the plane last night. He introduced himself, but didn't give his complete name, though he obviously knew who I was."

And he knew I was in charge of the project he'd vowed to sabotage, she added to herself, painfully aware she'd made a very bad start indeed, accusing the old man's son, whom he so obviously loved and admired.

Yet she was still angry enough to shift her gaze back to Duke Tyrell, wait with thrust-out chin for some acknowledgment that she spoke the truth.

"As a matter of fact, I *did* know," he said casually, turning to his father. "You see, I'd been up to Chicago to check on her."

Jenna's fury knew no bounds. "*Check* on me?" she spluttered, wishing at that moment she might tighten her hands about his tanned, good-looking throat.

To her surprise, Ed T. chuckled and gave his son a fond look. "So *that's* where you've been," he said. "And here I thought you'd gone chasing off with . . ."

He stopped and the two of them exchanged approving glances. Then, as if he'd just remembered Jenna's awkward position, the old man courteously sought to soothe her ire.

Yet he did it like a Tyrell. "You mustn't mind Duke," he said. "He's as smart and stubborn and ornery as he has a right to be, considering whom he got it from. But I'm still boss around here, and he won't give you a hard time unless I say so."

Her eyes flashed at the left-handed assurance of support. "I think I can guarantee that myself, Mr. Tyrell," she said with quiet determination, bringing her anger under control. "But, of course, I'll be grateful for your good offices."

"Call me Ed," he replied, his smile broadening as he bestowed a small measure of his approval on her. "Or Ed T., as most folks around here seem to do."

"All right."

Again she and Tom Courtenay—Duke Tyrell—were staring at each other with hostility, though his was tempered by amusement and some other quality she couldn't define.

"I'll leave you two alone to talk," Duke said shortly. "Since you're going to be staying with us—over my objections, I might add—I'll see you at dinner, Jenna Martin."

And with that challenge flung at her like a gauntlet he strode out of the room.

To think I let him kiss me, she thought, her cheeks burning as she looked after him. To think I actually wanted him to take me to bed.

The night before it had seemed as if Tom—*Duke Tyrell*—had truly found her attractive. Now she couldn't help thinking that he'd coldly embarked on a plan to discredit her.

What would he have done if I'd let him stay, she wondered—made love to me and then rolled out of bed in the morning to reveal his true identity and threaten me with the loss of my reputation if I didn't get on the next plane back to Chicago?

Of course, there had never been any real danger of that. To Jenna the whole notion of one-night stands with strangers was sordid, repugnant—even if, in Duke Tyrell's arms, her emotions might have betrayed her.

With a start, she realized the old man was watching her.

"Not telling his right name isn't the worst thing Duke's ever done," he said when he saw that he had her attention. "And I understand why he's acting this way. I haven't always led the most exemplary life either, and the boy loves me, wants to protect me from my sins."

"He's not exactly a boy anymore, is he?" Jenna replied, meeting and holding the old man's brown eyes.

"No, no," he said with obvious pride and the same soft chuckle she'd noted earlier. "Not hardly. Duke is just like me—so much it scares me sometimes. Except underneath he's got his mother's gentle streak."

"And her eyes?" Jenna was relaxing into her reporter's role, automatically beginning to put her subject at ease with small talk. "They're not yours either."

"No," said Ed T., for a moment a billion miles away. "Those are Mary's too."

Then he came to himself, seemed to remember that he was a famous figure with a reputation for courtesy and charm to uphold, and pressed a hidden buzzer behind his desk.

A moment later a woman who was probably the housekeeper appeared and Ed T. ordered what he called his "toothache medicine."

"Scotch," he explained to her with a wink. "When you're my age, you can claim a toothache any time of day. What'll you have, sweetheart?"

"Iced tea," she said promptly. "With lots of lemon."

He nodded his approval. "Most young women nowadays drink too much—like they were trying to be men," he said. "It's not becoming."

Expending a bit more effort than she would have expected, he got to his feet with the aid of a cane and ushered her over to the broad, curving chintz sofa that faced the lawns.

"Might as well be comfortable," he said, patting her knee as he sat beside her. "We can talk for an hour or so before I have to take my dad-blamed nap. Fire away."

Unobtrusively, Jenna took out her note pad. The hour passed quickly, with Ed T. sipping on his Scotch and "storying," as he put it, in response to her questions.

Not having read the contents of Paul's folder, she had chosen to begin with his memories of his father, Judge Sanford Tyrell, the patriarch who had founded the family's citrus and cattle empire.

And to her way of thinking the first interview went well. No deep truths, thought Jenna as she closed her notebook. Or heartfelt emotions yet. But a few good anecdotes I can use. She knew Ed T. Tyrell was still waiting to form an opinion of her and she must soft-pedal her curiosity, take her time if any real story were to emerge. Meanwhile he had been visibly wearied by their conversation. "Go ring the buzzer for Mrs. Haskins, sweetheart," he instructed her. "She can show you upstairs."

But Mrs. Haskins didn't appear. Instead a blond girl with Ed T.'s dark eyes came into the room. About nineteen years old and deeply tanned, she had a rounded body that was amply displayed by her brief tennis outfit.

"Hi," she said with a smile at Jenna. "Mrs. Haskins is setting the bread to rise. I'll take Miss Martin to her room, if you want."

"I'd appreciate it, sugar. Jenna, this pretty little thing is my granddaughter Caroline, my grandson Neddy's sister. Their daddy, my son Yancey . . . died some years ago."

He suddenly looked very old.

"But I've got the best granddaddy in the world," said Caroline Tyrell merrily, planting a resounding kiss on her grandfather's cheek.

Then she linked her arm with Jenna's, as friendly and guileless as a puppy.

"C'mon," she said. "I'll show you to your room. You can ask me all the questions you want."

In the hall outside Caroline lowered her voice. "Granddad was looking awfully tired," she said. "He has a bedroom on this floor now, next to his study. He can't manage stairs too well anymore and his heart isn't the best. His doctor makes him nap every afternoon."

Jenna shook her head. "I can't imagine anyone making a Tyrell do something against his will."

Caroline gave her a look. "Oh, well, that's the reputation we have, isn't it?" she said. "But we're . . . a bit more complicated than that."

Just then the phone rang shrilly.

"I'd better get that before Granddad does," she added hastily. "Anyway, it might be . . . someone for me. I'm expecting a call from Tallahassee. You can wait in the game room, if you'd like."

Indicating a door to Jenna's right that was ajar, Caroline hurried off down the hall to pick up the receiver. A moment later, she covered the mouthpiece and waved to Jenna. "It is my friend," she called, unable to hide her pleasure. "I'll only be a few minutes."

Hesitantly, Jenna opened the door of the game room.

Nobody was about. The room, fitted up with a bar, billiard table, and walls of books, had been adopted by someone as an office. A desk, as large as Ed T.'s but built of plain, heavy oak, held several orderly stacks of folders and papers, some ledgers, a leather cup of pencils, and a telephone.

Sinking into one of the overstuffed chairs that faced away from the door toward the billiard table, she began to flip through her notes. She didn't hear the step in the doorway.

"What do you think you're doing in here?" said Duke Tyrell tersely behind her. "This room is off limits."

Stung, she jumped to her feet and whirled to face him.

"I'm here at your cousin Caroline's invitation," she retorted haughtily. "Not to snoop, but to wait until she finishes her phone call so she can show me to my room. At least your cousin exhibits some semblance of Southern hospitality."

"Niece," corrected Duke, still in that hard voice he'd used with her for the first time in front of his father. "Caroline is my *niece.*"

But though he still seemed anything but welcoming, she caught a glint of amusement in his beautiful eyes. It only fueled her anger.

"My condolences to her in either case," she snapped. "Because you're the rudest man I've ever met."

And with that she attempted to walk past him out of the room. Calmly, imperturbably, he blocked her exit.

"You didn't think so last night, Jenna Martin," he drawled in a low voice, moving closer so that they were only a breath apart.

To her dismay, she found herself longing for his arms to come around her, awaiting with eager anticipation the pressure of that rough, tender mouth.

No, she thought. Not if I have any willpower left.

"I mistakenly thought you were a gentleman," she replied as coldly as she could. "That is, until you asked me . . ." She stopped, blushing, though she refused to drop her eyes before his insolent gaze.

"To *what?*" he asked. "Go to bed? Don't tell me that wasn't on your mind too."

All right, thought Jenna furiously. I wouldn't bother to lie to you anyway.

"Last night, I didn't ascribe any ulterior motives to your behavior, at least," she replied, avoiding his question. "But, when I think what you were really trying to do—to compromise me so I wouldn't be able to carry out my assignment . . ."

"So?" He gave a little shrug. "What if I was? I got less—and more—than I'd bargained for."

His voice had softened perceptibly on the word *more*, and, alive in every fiber to his male sensuality, she demanded shakily, "What do you mean?"

Duke gave her an unreadable look. "I'm not sure," he said. "Yet."

But though his half-formed thoughts were hidden from her, his mood was not. For the moment, he might be content to feel amused at her chagrin and hostility. But that could change, she knew, in an instant. It was clear that she brought out the predator in him; he would take her eventually, if he could.

"Anyway," he was saying, the mocking note back in his voice, "you're the one with the ulterior motive now, 'Jenna, sweetheart.' And, despite what my father said, you'd better be nice to me if you want to get a story here."

Without warning, then, his arms inexorably came around her, though she struggled to evade them. His mouth on hers, he pushed her lips apart with his strong, sweet tongue as if exploring already claimed territory. He pulled her close, bringing her soft curves up against a wall of hard muscle.

Angrily, she crushed down the unbidden response that seemed to arise from the deepest part of her being.

Scarcely able to breathe and trembling with the multitude of emotions his kiss was arousing, she groped about with one foot for the shape of an expensive leather boot. Locating it, she brought her stiletto heel down, hard, on his instep. He yelped in pain and surprise.

In that moment, she broke free and managed to step around him to the door.

"That's an example of just how nice I can be," she told him, eyes blazing. "And of exactly what you'll get if you dare to touch me again."

Muttering an oath, he reached for her, but she was too quick for him, ducking outside the door and shutting it quickly. She hurried off down the hall, ignoring Caroline Tyrell's frantic gestures.

At the end of the hall were tall, slim French doors and she stepped beyond them to find herself in a wicker-and-chintz-decorated sun porch surrounded by plants of every description.

"Well, hello, my dear," said an elderly woman's voice. Aunt Bliss.

"Hello," said Jenna, trying to smooth her countenance. "You must be Mrs. Sanford, Mr. Ed T.'s sister."

"Who else could I be?" The old woman chuckled. "Come 'round here and let me have a look at you. I want to see if women reporters are as scrappy as they say."

Obediently, Jenna came around to face the small, once-plump woman ensconced in the straw peacock chair. At first glance, Bliss Tyrell Sanford appeared soft, almost lethargic in her voile print dress. But though her puffy arms and lazy posture revealed a woman who had spent a sedentary life, the overall impression she gave was one of surprising curiosity, sympathy, and liveliness. Jenna felt an almost immediate liking for Duke Tyrell's aunt, sensing that she had found an ally.

"Well, ma'am?" she said, a smile warming her face. "Am I what you expected?"

"Call me Aunt Bliss." The old lady's brown eyes

42

sparkled. "As for your question, I'd say you are, in some ways . . . not a tough young woman, certainly, but hard to best. Am I right?"

Jenna's smile broadened. "I like to think so," she admitted. "But maybe you should ask your nephew."

"Duke?" The old woman raised her brows. "Has he been giving you trouble already?"

Jenna nodded ruefully. To her surprise, she found the whole story, with the exception of a few of the most intimate details, tumbling out. Aunt Bliss seemed to enjoy the account immensely as she listened with bright-eyed interest.

"I'm afraid he's earned himself a sore foot," Jenna concluded.

"Well, I love that boy, but it sounds like he deserved it."

"Richly." The deep voice in the doorway made Jenna flush with embarrassment. Incredibly, he had caught her gossiping with his aunt—*and about him.* Already her visit with the Tyrells was in a shambles and things were going from bad to worse.

She dared to meet his eyes.

"Let Aunt Bliss be my witness," he was saying in his softly accented voice. "I apologize for my behavior. I'm still opposed to the story, but you're right, I've been insufferably rude this afternoon."

Duke Tyrell telling her he was sorry? Jenna swallowed. "Let's forget it," she said.

He grinned. "When my foot stops hurting. By the way, you left this in my study."

One brow arching wickedly, he held out her leather envelope purse in tanned, lean fingers. "You know that's a symbolic gesture, don't you," he added, "for a woman to leave her purse in a man's private domain?"

And winking at his aunt, he turned with that panther grace of his and left them.

Jenna knew she must be blushing furiously. Aunt Bliss

gave her dry, throaty chuckle. "That's a Tyrell apology for you," she said. "They always come with a twist of lemon."

Jenna managed to laugh a little too. "Apparently so," she said. "I just wish someone would take me to my room so I don't have to run into Duke again before dinner."

"Dear me," said Aunt Bliss. "Where is Mrs. Haskins or that child, Caroline?"

Diffidently, Jenna explained.

"Well," said the older woman, getting to her feet with surprising agility. "In that case, I'll take you myself."

With relief, Jenna followed Bliss Sanford back to the flagstone entry and up the thickly carpeted stairs.

Her room was a delight, furnished with a delicate, high old mahogany four-poster and matching dresser, a pink seersucker spread, slipper chairs, and a chaise lounge in the same pink, rose-sprigged print as the wallpaper. Filmy curtains were pulled back from broad windows that overlooked the ranch's hazy blue-green vista.

"Why, it's lovely!" she exclaimed. "A charming room."

"It was my sister-in-law Elizabeth's," said Aunt Bliss.

"Oh?" Jenna frowned. "I thought her name was Mary."

The other woman shook her head. "No," she said. "That's a long story. I imagine you'll want to shower and change. Things are kept quiet around here while my brother naps. We dine at seven."

With a brief, welcoming squeeze of Jenna's hand, she moved to depart, then paused in the doorway. "By the way," she added, "maybe somebody should tell you—we're having other guests tonight. You might want to wear a long dress."

Wondering who the guests might be and still puzzling over who Mary was, Jenna slipped gratefully into the shower of her room's private bath. She would be living a life of luxury in a hornet's nest, she thought, letting the water stream down around her. Then, drying off with one of the thick towels monogrammed white on pale pink with a huge *T*, she slipped on her white terry robe and went to sit on the chaise lounge, opening her Tyrell folder.

Rena had compiled a summary sheet on each of the Tyrells. Guiltily, she selected Duke's first.

"Thomas Courtenay Tyrell, thirty-four, called 'Duke,'" the resume began, making Jenna long to have read it earlier. "A hunk."

Rena did have a way with words.

"Son of Mary Courtenay and Ed T. Tyrell. Probably conceived at the Tyrell Ranch but born in Charlotte, North Carolina. Lived in Asheville until the age of eight, at which time his mother died and he was adopted by his natural father. . . ."

Jenna's eyes opened wide in amazement. Duke Tyrell was illegitimate—a love child who'd been foisted on the rest of the family by a father who obviously cared for and needed him very much. *No wonder* he doesn't want the story written, Jenna thought with sudden compassion. I've seen at a glance how much he loves his father and I know he wants to protect Ed T. But now that he's been accepted by the rest of the clan, I can't blame him for wanting to prevent some reporter from digging around in the past to bring up his origins again. And how will he feel facing his business contacts and friends after the story comes out, even his nephew Neddy, who, without Duke in the picture, would have been Ed T.'s only male heir? I'll bet Neddy both admires and resents him, she guessed.

Soberly she read the rest of the little resume. It seemed Duke was hardly the uneducated rancher she'd supposed. With a bachelor's degree in agriculture from the University of Florida, he'd gone on to win a master's in business and his law degree at Harvard.

Clearly he'd been designated to become head of the family as Ed T.'s heir in power as well as fortune. Neddy, whom she saw had earned a bachelor's in business at Florida with "barely passing marks," as Rena put it, must certainly be jealous of that.

And his cousins—the sons of Ed T.'s two brothers, the late Burton Tyrell and Everett, who resided now in Texas. What did they think of that masterful interloper? Of that Rena had only noted Duke was "respected in the family for his business sense."

"A confirmed bachelor," she had added, "Duke Tyrell is also a lady-killer, the despair of Tampa's best society matrons and their sleek, well-brought-up daughters.

"Probably he's been to bed with each of the most liberal among the latter at least once. Current steady companion is an old flame who's recently been divorced, Victoria Howard, sister of Peter Howard, one of Duke's law partners.

"The affable Pete Howard is also divorced," Rena had added in pencil in the margin. "He might be a good source."

I wonder, thought Jenna, knifed by an absurd jealousy that she resolutely put from her, if it's Victoria and Peter Howard who are coming to dinner tonight.

Her hunch proved correct. At ten to seven Jenna came downstairs in a floor-length cotton lace Mexican "wedding gown" she'd bought on a trip to the Yucatan several years earlier. It was a favorite, worn to numerous patio and pool parties along the North Shore during the brief Chicago summers, a dress that made her feel both demure and glamorous.

On impulse, she had unbraided her waist-length hair and ironed it straight, so that it fell in a shining curtain about her shoulders.

A low whistle rewarded her from the bottom of the staircase, where a tanned man in his late twenties, with curly dark hair and Ed T.'s brown eyes, was watching her descend.

"Hi," he said with an ingratiating smile. "I'm Neddy, heir to my daddy's title of Tyrell black sheep. If you're an example of what reporters look like, then I demand to be interviewed!"

Taking his hand, she smiled at him uncertainly. From behind him came a little intake of breath. Duke had appeared, holding lightly to his father's elbow. With the two of them were a striking young woman with glittering green eyes and masses of curly dark auburn hair, almost the color of mahogany, and a tall, well-built young man with hair of a lighter rusty shade.

Unwillingly, she returned her gaze to Duke. His eyes, narrowed, were raking over her with obvious approval.

"Well, don't you look nice, Jenna, my dear," said Ed T., graciously taking her hand in turn. "These two young rascals are friends of mine—Vicki and Pete Howard. You two, this is Jenna Martin, my biographer."

"How do you do?" With a genuinely engaging grin Pete Howard also offered his hand.

His sister did not. Coolly her green gaze traveled from Jenna to Duke and back again. "A prizewinning writer, isn't that so?" she murmured. "I've been looking forward to meeting you so much."

The amenities observed, Ed T. offered Jenna his arm. "I'd be honored if you'd be my dinner partner, young lady," he said.

"I thought that was going to be my reward for paying you so much attention," said Vicki Howard with smooth, teasing sulkiness.

Ed T. loved it. "You know I don't want Duke jealous of me," the old man said, pinching her cheek.

As it turned out, Pete Howard partnered Caroline and Neddy his Great-aunt Bliss, while Vicki, looking as satisfied as a cat with cream, clung to Duke's strong arm. Jenna, however, seated at Ed T.'s right, was feeling far from satisfied at the arrangement. Duke said scarcely two words to her throughout the meal of roast beef, Florida sweet corn cut from the cob and scalloped with Apalachicola oysters, citrus and spinach salad, and Mrs. Haskins's scrumptious homemade bread.

She wasn't sure what she hated most when it came to Duke Tyrell—being ignored completely or suffering as the object of his mocking attention.

There was nothing mocking about the way he was regarding the lovely, confident Vicki, she noted. Instead he was being the gracious, charming Tom Courtenay she'd liked so well.

Meanwhile Ed T. had consumed several glasses of wine, preceded no doubt by a nip or two of "toothache medicine," and his tongue had loosened. By the time the dessert, a sponge cake with strawberries, was brought in, he was trading off-color jokes with Pete and Neddy.

"Ed, for heaven's sake," said Aunt Bliss affectionately. "You'll embarrass our guest."

"Nonsense." He patted Jenna's hand. "She's a reporter, even if she *is* the most ladylike one I've ever seen. What embarrasses her is when someone doesn't give her all the facts, like Duke last night."

Oh, no, thought Jenna. Here it comes. Out of the corner of her eye she saw Vicki pause in the midst of a remark to Duke and glance in her direction.

"Duke came back on the plane last night with Jenna and didn't tell her who he was," the old man continued, relishing the attention he'd attracted. "But I have to admit I'm disappointed in him," he added.

By now Duke's interest was also plain. "Is that so?" he asked, turning his aquamarine eyes in his father's direction.

The old man nodded, lighting a cigar to prolong the moment. "Now if that had been me, at your age," he said, regarding his son between puffs with that wicked, glinting Tyrell humor, "I'd have done more than *misinform* a pretty young lady like Jenna Martin. I'd have wined and dined her at Bern's and offered her a little proposition."

There was polite, indulgent laughter. Flushing, Jenna dared to meet Duke's eyes and saw he had reddened slightly under his tan.

"For all you know, I did," he replied with equanimity when the laughter had died away, then he glanced back at Jenna. "But Miss Martin is a lady of honor."

He had spoken soberly, almost respectfully, and she saw in him again the Tom Courtenay she had trusted instinctively the night before.

"And Duke Tyrell is a man of his word," she replied with sudden daring, aware the remark would cause some speculation.

"Well," said Caroline with a little laugh, "there seems to be more here, don't y'all think, than meets the eye?"

Ed T. chuckled softly and puffed on his cigar without retort. He seemed as satisfied as if some purpose, hidden until now, had been accomplished, Jenna thought.

Now I know what Uncle Gene meant by *wily*, she thought, watching the old man with sudden admiration. He's a fox—not the least bit inebriated at all. He wants Duke to cooperate with me and so he attacks me in that charming way of his and relies on Duke's natural chivalry to prod him to my defense.

After supper, she sat on the porch with Pete and Neddy and Aunt Bliss. Ed T. had gone to his room to lie down and watch a favorite television program, and Caroline, Duke, and Vicki had disappeared. Probably Duke and Vicki were kissing on the terrace, she thought. Or worse.

A few moments later Duke and Vicki came in together, confirming her suspicions, and then Vicki and Pete were making their good-byes. They were on their way to the family horse farm near Ocala to sign the legal papers that would add four hundred acres to their holdings, Pete explained. But they would stop by on their way back home.

I can hardly wait, Jenna thought, shaking back her straight silky hair as she stood on the veranda with Duke and Neddy and wished the Howards good-bye.

"Beautiful night for a walk in the moonlight," said Neddy at Jenna's elbow as they watched the Howards'

Lincoln move off down the long driveway. "We could start on our interview, if you want."

"Sorry," said Duke. "But Jenna and I are going for a ride and you aren't invited." Somehow he had managed to lay his hands on Jenna's cashmere stole and now he settled it lightly about her shoulders, lifting her hair aside in the process.

"You'll need this," he added matter-of-factly. "I have the top down."

She turned toward him slightly, her mouth open a little, and saw his eyes gleaming at her, daring her to accept.

But "Hadn't we better be going?" was all he said.

The nerve of him! she thought in amazement. Yet, even while she was thinking it, some perverse spirit in her made her meekly accept the arm Duke offered, saying softly to Neddy, "I guess our interview will have to wait."

Then they were walking side by side to the family's rambling garage and he was seating her courteously again in his luxurious automobile. A moment later they had shot off down the drive, bathed in cool night air with a canopy of stars over their heads.

Incredibly, after all that had happened between them that day, she was riding off into the dark, to God knew where, with the fatally attractive, exasperating, and sometimes gentle Duke Tyrell beside her.

4

As they drove, her hair streamed out behind her, then whipped back into her face. With one hand, he reached over and tucked it carefully under the shawl again.

"I hate to do that," he remarked. "You have absolutely the most beautiful hair I have ever seen."

"Thank you." She felt absurdly pleased at his compliment. Consciously she willed herself to remember that Rena had said this man had slept with most of Tampa's willing debutantes. Of course, Rena was prone to exaggerate. But she mustn't start making allowances for him just because he could be so warm and demanding and his firm masculine body was so disturbingly near.

"I don't suppose you would let me put an arm around you," he said softly, breaking into her thoughts.

"I don't suppose."

"Well . . . hold my hand, then."

He laid his hand, palm up, provocatively in her lap. She was forced to take it to avoid even greater liberties, and he laced his fingers warmly through her own.

"That's better," he said. "I like touching you."

Is this just another plan to get me to drop the story? she longed to ask even as the skin of her palm and in between her fingers tingled. She felt delightfully vulnerable to his touch. But she knew she couldn't pose the question without destroying a mood she confessed to herself she wanted to preserve.

"Where are we going?" she asked instead.

"To visit a tree house," he replied cryptically in a tone

that told her he wouldn't elaborate. "It's a bit of a drive. Don't you think your head would be more comfortable on my shoulder? You could count the stars in the Dipper, gaze up at the moon . . ."

Maybe it's the power of suggestion, Jenna thought, but suddenly that's exactly what I'd like to do. Then she remembered what he'd been doing with Vicki Howard less than an hour before and felt like a fool.

"If you'd let go of my hand now and lay yours on my knee," he was saying practically, "I could just slide my arm around you."

Instead she removed his hand from her lap and drew back into herself. "You're really something," she said. "One woman after dinner and another for a nightcap. But you can count me out of your lineup."

"What in hell do you mean?" Abruptly he slowed the sleek progress of the Mercedes and pulled onto a grassy shoulder.

For a moment they sat regarding each other like combatants in the pale moonlight.

"Vicki Howard on the terrace," she explained in a small voice, half ashamed at what certainly sounded like jealousy. She wondered suddenly if she'd been mistaken.

He frowned. "What about Vicki?" he asked, and then shook his head in disbelief. "You think I was out there making love to her, don't you?" he said.

She nodded dumbly.

"I hope you don't make the same kind of assumptions in your reporting. Vicki and I *and Caroline* were visiting with my father in his room."

Jenna winced at the censure in his voice and knew she deserved it.

"I . . . I'm sorry," she whispered. "It's my turn to apologize to you."

He said nothing for a moment, looking not at her but straight ahead at the tree-shadowed highway, his hands, strong and brown in the moonlight, resting on the Mercedes' leather wheel cover.

Tentatively, she reached out to touch his arm. "Please don't turn around and go back," she added, certain she had read his intention correctly. "I want to see your tree house, whatever it is. And I'd . . . be glad to have your arm around me."

For a moment then his beautiful eyes searched her face. "All right," he said finally. "If you mean that."

She nodded her assent.

Shifting gears, he pulled back onto the highway and drew her into the circle of his arm. Her cheek against his velvety corduroy sport coat, Jenna became intimately aware of the mingled scents she'd noticed before: pipe tobacco, mossy after-shave, and the aroma of his own skin, tonight just faintly laced with musk.

"I really would like it if you'd put your hand on my knee," he reminded her in that deep, soft voice with its trace of a Southern accent. "But I won't insist."

A bit hesitantly, she complied. The effect of his hard muscle and sinew and bone, shifting under his superbly tailored trouser leg as he routinely adjusted his pressure on the gas pedal, was electric to her senses.

He's like a great dangerous tiger, she thought—one that I can't help wanting to embrace. Here we are, sworn adversaries when it comes to my project, and I'm in real peril of succumbing to his charm. Yet, like an idiot, I feel perfectly safe.

With a little sigh, she relaxed against him.

"That's better," he said again, the words muffled a little by her hair. "I won't eat you alive. You know, for a smooth Yankee from the big city, sometimes you don't act very sophisticated."

Not sure if he was implying her behavior was an act or if he was genuinely puzzled over the discrepancy between his preconceived image of her and the reality, she didn't reply.

To her surprise, he switched on the radio, selecting an FM station that played classical music. They drove awhile with only the sound of the music interrupting the moonlit silence of the night. Then finally Duke was turning off the main highway down a side road. Moments later he guided the Mercedes through an open iron gate and up a steep narrow lane that cut through a jungle of trees and vegetation.

Jenna sat up a bit to improve her view. "What is this place?" she asked. "It looks like a private estate."

He gave her a quick glance. "The owner's hardly ever here."

"But that's trespassing."

He didn't reply. At the top of what seemed a very high hill for Florida, they passed through another quaint, lacy iron gate that arched overhead, and then the big old white wooden house that was the heart of the property came into plain view.

Deep, cool-looking verandas shaded both stories on at least three sides. Floor-to-ceiling windows were trimmed and shuttered in a dark color, probably a forest green, that matched the steeply pitched roof. She noted two tall chimneys.

Huge old live oaks that must have seen Civil War days dotted the lawns, their Spanish moss swaying in the faint breeze with ghostly grace. She could smell newly cut grass, blossoms somewhere. A mockingbird called out, sweetly talkative.

Duke halted the car before they reached the gravel turnaround in front of the house, parking in the shadow of a big, glossy-leaved magnolia with silvery pale lichens splotching its trunk. He turned quietly to look at her.

"It's a beautiful old place," she said, gazing again at the house even as she wondered if a caretaker would approach momentarily with a shotgun. "So . . . serene —like a haven somehow. And yet . . . it has an *expectant* air."

She paused. "Is this what you mean by a tree house?"

"No." Still his eyes didn't leave her face. "I knew I was right to bring you here," he said at last.

She turned to him then, a question on her face, and he shook his head slightly, as if to say he wouldn't answer it—yet.

"C'mon," he said, getting out and coming around to open the door for her. "I'll show you exactly what I meant."

Taking her hand, he led her across the lawn at an angle to the house, toward a break in the thicket of trees that surrounded the old mansion's sweeping lawns on every side. As they approached, she could see in the bright moonlight that they were on a very high hill indeed. Below, night-darkened ridges and valleys stretched away. In the distance a radio or water tower blinked with light to ward off low-flying planes.

"Why it's almost like a mountaintop!" Jenna exclaimed. "You'd think you were in Tennessee. I didn't know there were such places here."

"Holly Hill has the third highest elevation in the state."

He was smiling at her in the shadows, guiding her to rickety, slanting wooden steps that seemed to lead up into an enormous, vine-twisted oak.

"Lift your skirt a little," he advised, setting one foot on the first step. "The view is better from up above."

Obediently hitching up her skirt with one hand and holding fast to Duke with the other, Jenna confidently mounted the shaky staircase, emerging with him on a high wooden platform. The view of the valley below, washed in moonlight and splashed with the shadows of clouds, was nothing short of spectacular.

"Oh, *Duke*. . . ." she breathed, unconsciously addressing him for the first time by his family nickname. "It's wonderful."

He slipped one arm casually about her. "Careful of the railing," he said. "Splinters." And then: "It really *is* a power spot, isn't it?"

"Oh, yes."

They stood that way, arms naturally about each other,

just looking out before them, listening to the mockingbird vary his serenade.

She felt again the warmth and sense of connection that had pulsed so powerfully between them before. At the moment it was a quiet feeling, yet profound, full of a tingling awareness of what might happen if they moved or spoke.

After some minutes, his fingers tightened on her waist. "I'd really like to kiss you again," he said wryly, "if you'd promise not to stamp on my foot."

Frowning slightly, she looked up at him. "Does it still hurt?"

He nodded. "There's even a little bruise."

"Oh, I *am* sorry. . . ."

"Never mind. I was being boorish and arrogant. I can be sometimes."

"Yes," she said with a rueful little smile. "I know."

The corners of his mouth turned down slightly. "Well?" he asked. "May I trust there will be no painful repercussions?"

Though she did not answer, her lips parted softly in reply.

"I believe I'll take my chances," he said, lowering his mouth to hers.

At first, his kiss was gentle, as each explored without haste the flavor and texture of the other. His tongue entered her mouth again, sweetly, diffidently. When she did not protest—when in fact she welcomed it—he began to probe with a mounting urgency.

It would be this way if she let him make love to her, she guessed—first the sweet invasion, filling her with the warmth and completeness she craved, and then surrender, because he would brook no less. Her arms full of his hard tall body, she embraced him eagerly, longing to surround and enfold him in the most intimate way possible, to open herself without reservation.

It was what he wanted from her, she knew. One strong

capable hand was in her hair, but the other molded itself
to the small of her back, forcing her body to accommodate his so that she could feel the telltale outline of his
passion.

How I ache to have him, she thought, as her body
responded to his need. Never had she been kissed by a
man like this one before, never had she wanted one so
much. Not even in bed had Paul been able to make her
feel such longing.

Finally he drew back to look at her, his eyes glittering
in the dark.

I thought we would be enemies, she said to herself in
amazement. But we're like lovers. I want to give him
everything I have.

"Duke," she whispered before she could stop herself,
the words seeming to spring from some well of truth-
telling she could not suppress. "Kiss me again."

He needed no second prompting. Lifting her off her
feet, he held her so that her breasts were crushed against
his upper chest and her mouth was a breath above his.
Her hair fell in a curtain about his face.

"Kiss *me*, Jenna," he said with fierce, quiet urging.

Caught in the splendor of the moment, she put her
mouth on his, did with her tongue what he had done—
explored, plumbed, caressed.

Time seemed to stand still as his warm mouth welcomed her. Rough and virile, his tongue moved against
her own. Then, overwhelmed at what she was feeling,
she gave him several soft, shy little kisses that just
brushed his mouth and hid her face in his shoulder.

"Oh, my God, Jenna," he groaned, his deep voice
catching with emotion. "The way you can make me want
you. . . . Sweetheart, I don't know what we're going to
do."

Gently he set her on her feet and looked down at her,
though he still imprisoned her in his arms.

"Do about what?" she asked shakily.

"The way I keep wanting to touch you and kiss you. The way you kiss me back." He paused. "You know where it will lead."

I know and I don't care, she wanted to reply. We'll be lovers, tangled up in the bedclothes.

But she answered him lightly. "It won't do for sworn enemies to be seen kissing and hugging in dark corners."

"Not so much that. I'm still opposed to your being here—at least as far as the story is concerned. But I want to fight fair."

"Don't worry. I'm not going to drop the project."

They looked at each other for a moment.

"Will you kiss me again anyway?" he asked. "Even if it makes me want to undress you and take you into the house?"

She drew in her breath, stabbed by desire at the mental picture his words evoked.

"How . . . could you do that?"

A muscle twitched alongside his mouth. "I have the key."

"But . . ."

"It's *my* house, Jenna. I've owned it since I was eight years old. It used to belong to my mother."

"Mary Courtenay owned this place?"

"So you know the story. I might have guessed."

"Only a little." Lightly, her fingers traced the soft edge of his lapel even as she felt him recede from her.

He didn't reply.

"Do you want to tell me?" she asked.

"For publication? Or off the record?"

Now it was her turn to hesitate. "Not the latter," she said finally. "I'll only have to ask someone else."

Duke winced. "I'd rather not hear about that. Ed T. is old. He doesn't know what he's doing, opening this up again."

Pain was clear in his voice, and though she was partly responsible for it, she longed to make it go away.

"It must have been a beautiful relationship between the two of them," she said, "here in this lovely place."

"It *was* beautiful. But who will believe it when it's plastered across the pages of your magazine?"

Stung, she recoiled from his words, trying not to show her own hurt.

"I don't write stories like that," she told him. "I thought you were going to kiss me again."

"No." He dropped his hands and then touched her waist to guide her down the stairs. "Let's go back to the car."

As they walked back slowly across the lawns that were so redolently fresh cut and wet with dew, she tried to imagine the unknown Mary Courtenay. She could see her and Ed T. walking there in the moonlight. Probably she had worn jasmine in her hair. But Jenna couldn't picture Duke's mother's face.

With a certain restraint, he settled her again in the car and got in beside her.

"You see how awkward this is going to be?" he asked.

"Yes," she whispered. "I see."

Duke started the car and they took off with a swish of gravel down the narrow drive. Suddenly he gathered her back into the circle of his arm.

"Then come here," he said roughly, smoothing her tucked lace gown, her hair. "We might as well make the best of it."

On the way back they didn't talk. Jenna was afraid to guess what Duke might be thinking. Instead she simply allowed herself to feel his arm about her, his fingers tracing the pattern of her sleeve or her skirt where it lay across her thigh.

As a reporter, she was supposed to be a skeptic, and she knew that, theoretically, at least, she couldn't be sure he wasn't just using his considerable charm again to sabotage her assignment. But she didn't believe that. He would fight fair, as he'd said. And he wanted her. That much was clear. It was no act, and the way she reciprocated his desire evoked little shivers of fear and delight.

Don't forget what Rena said about him, she warned herself. He's a confirmed bachelor and he wants to have an *affair* with you—an honorable affair, certainly, but that's all.

Her warning was to no avail. A minute later, she could not resist laying her head on his shoulder in a soft little gesture of trust.

"Jenna," he said simply, with some amazement, and tightened his embrace.

Later, as they approached the Bar-T gate, he seemed to withdraw again a little. In front of the main house veranda he kissed her briefly and almost impersonally, then leaned across her to open the car door.

"Don't wait up for me," he said, his eyes unreadable. "We've got a mare ready to foal any day now and I want to check on her progress. Anyway, Ed T. gets up early and he'll expect you to interview him again."

"All right." She got out and smoothed back her hair. "Good night, Duke."

"Good night."

With a purring growl, the Mercedes shot forward, toward the garage. Not wanting to be caught looking after him, she turned quickly and went into the house.

Ed T. was already at the table in the family's airy, bamboo-decorated breakfast room when she came down at seven the following morning.

"Well, well, young lady," he said, "I didn't expect to see you so early. Matter of fact, I planned to have a look at some things around the ranch this morning. Forgive me if I don't pull out your chair."

Jenna smiled at him. "It's the thought that counts," she said. "Why didn't you expect to see me?"

His brown eyes twinkled at her as Mrs. Haskins's assistant, a young woman with a Spanish accent who had helped out with their dinner the night before, brought in juice and fresh coffee, uncovered dishes of eggs and grits and bacon.

"You were out so late with that boy of mine," he replied.

She felt herself blushing faintly and hoped he wouldn't notice. The young assistant housekeeper, who wore a distracted and pensive expression, was paying scant attention to their conversation.

"I . . . guess Duke and I have buried the hatchet," Jenna told the old man finally. "And not in each other this time. I suppose you could say we've agreed to disagree."

Hungrily, she dished out eggs and bacon with a liberal hand, then pleased Ed T. by taking some of the buttery, bland grits.

"My father came from Georgia, as you might remember, and we used to have these now and then," she explained.

Ed T. nodded. "Did y'all take in a movie?" he asked with flat curiosity.

Jenna lowered her lashes in amusement. "No," she said, sipping her tall glass of freshly squeezed juice before finishing her answer. "As a matter of fact, Duke took me to see Holly Hill. We even climbed into the tree house."

She glanced up to catch the old man's surprise.

"Why . . . you must be somebody special, sugar," he said in that dry, humorous voice of his. "Duke's never taken any of his girls out there—at least, not that I know of."

Her large hazel eyes widened at his words before she lowered them, unwilling to admit her absurd pleasure.

"I hardly qualify as one of 'Duke's girls,'" she retorted with an uneasy little laugh.

Ed T. chuckled and buttered himself a biscuit. "Don't be too sure about that, honey," he said. "You will, if you get under his skin."

Thoroughly embarrassed, Jenna thanked her lucky stars when Caroline bounced in a moment later. The young blonde planted a kiss on her grandfather's cheek and began to chatter about returning to Tallahassee for the new term. Some friends from Sarasota, she explained, would pick her up about dinnertime.

"But I'll be back to help celebrate your birthday, Granddad," she assured him, helping herself to eggs and coffee.

Have I gotten under Duke's skin? Jenna wondered, absenting herself from their conversation and staring out the breakfast room window. Last night, at the tree house, it had seemed so, though he had retreated into a kind of nonchalance or indifference on their return to the Bar-T.

As for herself, she had to admit it: the tall scion of the Tyrell family, despite his reputation as a heartbreaker and his opposition to her project, had turned her head. She had been able to think of nothing else as she'd tossed in the antique four-poster bed. Remembering what he'd hinted he'd like to do with her, she had been completely unable to sleep last night.

Just then, Duke's Mercedes backed out of the garage and shot down the ranch's long approach lane toward the highway.

Caroline followed her glance. "He was awfully good with the foal last night, Jenna," she said. "You should've seen him."

"Oh, no," said Jenna. "It was born and I didn't get to watch."

"You can see her this morning. She's beautiful."

Then Wayne Keeper was arriving, to take Ed T. out to the barn in the golf cart he used now for jaunts in the vicinity of the ranch house. Caroline and Jenna were left alone.

"If Duke was up all night with the foal, I wonder why he's taking off in such a hurry this morning," said Jenna meditatively. "You'd think he'd want to get some sleep."

By now Caroline's mouth was full of biscuits and

marmalade. "I imagine he does," she said. "That's what *I'm* going to do. But he's got court this morning."

"Court?" Jenna's forehead furrowed in a frown.

"He's got a law practice in Tampa. Didn't you know?"

"I . . . knew about his law degree," Jenna replied. "But I didn't realize . . ."

She said nothing more, resolving not to bring up Duke Tyrell again except in the context of her story. Otherwise it would seem he was her only topic of conversation.

Gradually, Jenna became aware that the young Spanish-speaking assistant housekeeper was hurrying them.

Caroline had noticed it too. "Is anything wrong, Rosalia?" she asked.

"No, miss, nothing," said the young woman, who had dark hair and a pretty oval face. "Today Paco comes home from the hospital."

Eyes shiny wet with tears, Rosalia disappeared into the kitchen.

"Paco is her little brother," Caroline explained. "He has leukemia and he's been very ill. He's . . . not expected to live much longer."

Before Jenna could reply, Rosalia returned and began to clear the table.

"Is there anything I can do?" Caroline asked her softly.

"No." Rosalia's tears spilled, making Jenna want to hug her. "Not unless you can make Christmas come again in January. You see, Paco was so sick last month, he doesn't remember it. Now that he is feeling a little better—though it is a false betterness—it's all he asks about. They have given him less than a month."

With that, Rosalia was sobbing and Jenna had risen to put both arms about her.

"Isn't there something we could do?" she asked Caroline. "It shouldn't be so difficult to wrap some presents, put up a tree . . ."

"We always have Christmas at Aunt Bliss's house, down on Ballast Point," said Caroline. "Everything is there." Then she brightened. "But the Rogers Christmas House in Brooksville is famous! They'll have everything we need!"

"Well?" Jenna gave Rosalia a squeeze. "What are we waiting for?"

"Not a darn thing," said Caroline. "Let's go!"

Leaving a note to tell Ed T. where they'd gone, Jenna and Caroline set off five minutes later in the rental car for the cluster of old homes in Brooksville that had been converted into a kind of commercial Christmas fairyland. Except for December 25, Caroline told her, the so-called "Christmas House" was open every day in the year.

In an orgy of buying that put quite a dent in Jenna's checking account, they assembled the makings of a party that would surpass little Paco Nuñez's wildest dreams. When they returned to the ranch, it was with a silvery eight-foot artificial tree, multicolored lights, tiny hand-made ornaments in wood and glass and metal that depicted all manner of storybook characters, and even a music box that played Christmas carols in tinkling, bell-like tones. And, of course, there was also a huge shopping bag of gaily wrapped presents.

With Wayne Keeper's help and the tearful but enthusiastic assistance of Rosalia Nuñez, they got everything set up in the Nuñezes' modest but neatly kept bungalow. Paco's father, Caroline had told her, was the Bar-T's mechanic and maintenance man.

Jenna had a lump in her throat when the boy Paco arrived in the company of his parents to be carried inside. He was so painfully thin, so ravaged by his disease and the harsh, desperate treatments that had been used to no avail. But she felt a surge of happiness, too, at the flame of joy that leaped up in the child's luminous dark eyes when he saw the presents and the glowing tree.

As they sang carols together, with Ed T.'s bass providing a raspy accompaniment, and watched the boy open his packages, Jenna wasn't sure whether the tears that traced her cheeks denoted joy or sorrow. If only Duke were here, she thought.

It was just Ed T. and Jenna at supper, after Caroline's departure. Duke had not returned and no one seemed to expect him. Nor was there any sign of Neddy, and Aunt Bliss, Mrs. Haskins had informed her, would be spending the next few days at her home in town. She, Jenna, was invited for brunch the day after tomorrow.

Realizing she must put in some work if the story on Ed T. was to be completed on time, Jenna—with his permission—went for her notebook and tape recorder. She spent nearly an hour and three-quarters interviewing him at the table. Finally she called a halt, sensing the old man's weariness. She visited him briefly in his room as he settled down for his nightly dose of television.

The house grew quiet. Pausing for only a moment on the sun porch, Jenna stepped out onto the terrace, cool now under the stars.

There was no sign of Duke's cream-colored Mercedes on the drive. Walking down to the pool, she scooped up a handful of the chlorine-scented water, then let it run through her fingers. Heated for Caroline's swims, the water was much warmer than the air, quite pleasant to the touch.

On impulse, Jenna hurried upstairs to change. After all, she thought, I've swum in Lake Michigan on lots of days as cool as this.

After rummaging through her drawers, she selected her white string bikini and quickly put it on. Almost indecently brief, it had elicited wolf whistles on the swim deck of her Chicago apartment building the previous summer. But no one—especially not Duke with his turquoise bedroom eyes—would be there to see.

It'll be all right, she thought. I won't even turn on the lights.

Outside the surface of the huge swimming pool was

like hammered silver in the moonlight. Her long blond-streaked hair pulled back into a single braid, Jenna dove in with precision grace. She swam about for a few minutes, using some of the water ballet movements she'd learned in her college days.

Lost in the physical movement, she swerved and arched and plunged, wanting only to stretch and use her body, to resolve and relieve its tensions. Suddenly, strong arms came about her, viselike, and she was being pulled under the surface of the water, down, down to the bottom of the pool, where she was held tightly against a hard, aroused male body and thoroughly, passionately kissed.

5

Could it be Neddy? she wondered in the split second after she was grabbed. But she knew who it was, all right, in less than a moment. There was only one mouth like that, capable of touching her very soul.

Her captor released her and she shot like an arrow to the surface, blowing out her breath in a little trail of bubbles. They broke the water together.

"Duke!" she exclaimed, before he clapped a hand over her mouth.

"Hush," he said. "Ed T.'s asleep. And I don't want anybody else running down here. Now, what were you going to say?"

He took his hand away so that she could speak again as they treaded water together, but he kept one arm clasped around her. Duke's dark hair, wet, was slicked to his head, making him look like a thirties movie star. His light, darkly fringed eyes were glinting at her. In the moonlight she could see the powerful, glistening ripple of his shoulders, the muscles of his upper arms. Something in her went weak at the sight.

"Cat got your tongue?" he inquired pleasantly in that maddening way of his, adding softly, "That's not much of a suit you're wearing. But I like it."

"You could have drowned me, sneaking up on me like that," she spluttered, unwilling that he should know just how devastating an effect he had on her.

"Not the way you swim, sweetheart. You're a little naiad, aren't you?"

In reply, she slithered from his grasp and ducked underwater again, eluding him, to come up several feet away. But in a few powerful strokes, he caught her, pinning her to the side of the pool about midway along its length.

"Duke . . ." she began, breathless.

"You know you want me to kiss you again," he said, pushing her halfhearted opposition aside and bringing his mouth down on hers.

A passionate current passed between them at the contact, creating a surge of warmth inside her. The length of his tall, powerful body was pressing her into the side of the pool. Crushed as she was between him and the smooth tiles, she could feel his every outline, the surging muscles and hard desire.

Without actually deciding to do so, she slipped her arms around him, inviting him to press closer still. In her mouth his tongue was like a flame, touching off little brush fires of longing.

Eyes closed and lips parted, she moaned softly as his kisses spilled over onto her neck and shoulders. One sure brown hand had untied the strings of her bikini bra almost before she knew what he was doing. It floated away. Her bare breasts firmed and swelled, her nipples hardening at his touch and at their exposure to the cool night air.

"God, but you're lovely," he whispered, his mouth closing over one breast's peak.

The sensation of his tongue on her was exquisite as he traced narrowing concentric circles about one nipple before tugging at it with sweet, insistent demand. Cupping her other breast, he caressed its captured softness with his thumb.

"Duke, you mustn't," she pleaded, and then contradicted her words by cradling his dark head with unsteady hands.

"Why not?" he murmured, not taking his mouth away.

"Don't you like it? Haven't you ever made love in the water?"

There was a movement on the terrace, as if someone who had taken a step nearer to observe them more closely had accidently knocked into a lawn chair. Panic flooded her and she tried to wrench away. Protectively, Duke straightened to shield her, held her close against him.

"It's Neddy," he whispered, glancing over his shoulder. "I caught the glow of his cigarette just then. Keep still. He knows we're kissing, but he can't see that you're topless."

She collapsed against him, sinking a little in the water to hide her face in his shoulder. My reputation is in shreds, she thought. I might as well pack and go home. I wonder if Duke planned it this way.

Meanwhile Duke was holding her quietly, his strength a refuge.

"He's still there, damn him," he said after a moment. "C'mon. Swim to the deep end with me. Talk—loudly enough so that your voice will carry."

Incredibly, she was able to do as he suggested, to swim half naked beside him, parting the water with smooth easy strokes as she told him of seeing the foal, the party she and Caroline had arranged for Paco Nuñez.

"I heard about that from Wayne," he said as they reached the wall under the diving board. "It was a beautiful thing for you to do. Now turn around and back to the other end."

By the time they had reached shallow water again, they could hear Neddy's footsteps, retreating into the house. Weak with relief, Jenna sank down in the water on her knees. Duke knelt beside her to shelter her tenderly in his arms.

"I'm sorry, sweetheart," he told her, his hands cradling her back, his deep voice genuinely apologetic. "I didn't mean to let you in for that. It's been a tough twenty-four hours for me, and I . . . just started out to be playful, forgot where we were . . .''

The way a panther is playful, she thought, forced to admit that she too had wanted to frolic, with this dangerous, loving man for a partner. Her evasive maneuvers had been nothing but thinly disguised invitation. Even her initial reaction on discovering his presence had been searing, uninhibited delight.

With a start, she remembered that she wore nothing save her brief bikini bottom. Her breasts were pressed firmly against his mat of silky dark chest hair.

I wish what was happening between us could have gone on to its natural conclusion, she owned to herself shakily. A keen awareness of his masculine power, latent now but so close against her, returned to overwhelm her.

But it was too late. Cold reason had entered in. And she was not the sort to be just "one of Duke's girls," to let him undress her and make love to her any time he chose. She willed herself to composure.

"I wasn't trying to ruin your reputation this time," he was saying against her ear. "Just going after what I wanted. Please say something."

The thought that he had meant to embarrass her had crossed her mind and she regretted it now in the face of his obvious sincerity. "I . . . I'm not mad at you," she said, and then shivered a little. "I don't suppose you could find my top."

Briefly, he surveyed the pool. "Not without turning on the lights," he admitted. "I'll have to retrieve it for you in the morning—before Neddy does."

"I'd appreciate it very much if you'd look the other way while I get into my robe."

Her ardent response to him only a few minutes before had been anything but a secret. And so, held as she still was, half naked in his arms, the request sounded impossibly prim. He gave her a glinting, sardonic look.

"I think we're a bit past that, don't you?" he asked,

letting go of her and climbing out of the pool. "I'll get it for you."

Taking her white terry robe from the chaise lounge where she'd tossed it, he held it open with a racy, wicked little smile. She stared at him in consternation, unwillingly noting that his swimming trunks, cut to reveal the stunning build of his gorgeous, tall body, were nearly as brief as her own suit.

"C'mon, Jenna," he said softly, daring her.

Thus challenged, she got to her feet and came up the ladder, her teeth chattering with the cold. She was all too cognizant of his gleaming, narrowed gaze raking over her skin.

"Botticelli's Venus," he whispered, wrapping the robe snugly about her. "I wish I could take you up to my bed."

She pulled away, turning to face him.

"Please don't say things like that, even if you mean them," she said. "I was wrong to want to . . . *play* with you here. I'm a guest. Your father's hospitality . . ."

His eyes acknowledged her admission that she'd wanted to cooperate.

"Ed T. wouldn't mind," he said. "In fact, he'd approve."

She shook her head. "It's not the ethical thing to do."

Neither of them said anything more for a moment. Jenna could see gooseflesh prickling his skin, though he didn't shiver. God, but he's a beautiful man, she thought, longing to smooth the little bumps with her fingers. The way his chest hair grows down in an inverted triangle toward his swimming trunks . . . Again she longed to know the mystery and power of him, firsthand.

"I hate to broach this now," she said, almost wishing he would clap his hand over her mouth again. "But I have to interview you. Do you have any free time tomorrow?"

Instantly she could feel him recede from her. He bent to pick up the towel she'd brought and tossed it lightly over her shoulders.

71

"I have to go into Dade City," he said, his eyes unreadable now. "We're interested in a zoning matter that's before the county commission."

She could feel her reporter's heels digging in. "You have to eat, don't you? I could meet you somewhere."

He didn't make any teasing remarks about her asking him out to lunch. "I'm . . . not sure I'm ready to be interviewed," he said with a frown.

"Well, I understand how you feel. But Ed T. said he wants you to do it. He told me that you promised you'd cooperate."

The words sounded manipulative even to her own ears. In the moonlight his eyes seemed to appraise her.

"If you want, you can answer 'no comment' to all my questions," she added lightly, hating herself. "That way, we'll each have done our duty."

"All right." His voice betrayed no emotion. "Crest Cafe, at noon. I . . . think it's time we went up to the house."

They entered through the sun porch. Neddy was sitting there, watching television, idly twirling a glass of pale amber liquid.

"Have a pleasant swim?" he asked, with a lift of one eyebrow that created a striking, if transitory, family resemblance between the two men.

Duke did not reply.

"It was a little cold," said Jenna matter-of-factly. "But not bad if you kept your shoulders underwater."

Without waiting for further gambits from Ed T.'s grandson, she avoided his knowing dark gaze and walked ahead of Duke down the long hall and up the stairs. This time he didn't even kiss her good night.

"See you tomorrow, then," he said, casually going into his room and shutting the door.

It wouldn't surprise me, thought Jenna as she dried off in her little bathroom and slipped a nightgown over her head, to learn that he wouldn't have me in his bed now, whether or not I wanted it that way.

Despite the warnings she'd gotten before coming to the Bar-T, she had never realized what a challenge this assignment would be. Nor had she guessed how treacherous she'd find her own emotions when dealing with Duke Tyrell.

The Crest Cafe was situated on Dade City's main street, fronting on the town square with its big old courthouse. It was anything but fancy.

Arriving early, Jenna sipped iced tea and watched from a booth as the lunch crowd began to settle in: lawyers in their fastidious pinstriped suits, gaggles of secretaries, staffers from the county clerk's office in their shirtsleeves, an assortment of local politicians and their cronies. She glimpsed a reporter, bearded and corpulent and nonchalant, carrying his slim notebook and the stub of a pencil.

Gradually activity around the salad bar increased. The middle-aged waitresses in their white oxfords and short green checked dresses brought plastic drinking glasses of ice water and cellophane-encased menus or made quick trips from the kitchen with armloads of steaming luncheon specials on thick crockery plates.

At last Duke walked in, still in conversation with some other men whom she guessed were county commissioners. He was wearing a beautifully tailored tan cord suit and a white shirt open at the throat. And there was no one in the little cafe who could hold a candle to him.

Pausing for a moment to make a point, he surveyed the room and let his eyes rest on her briefly. Then, nodding in her direction, he disengaged himself from the others and came over to her.

"Hello," he said politely, sliding into the seat across from her, his long legs barely fitting under the Formica-topped table. He seemed anything but glad to see her. "Have you been waiting long?"

"Only a few minutes."

"I suppose we should decide on something. The barbecue here is good."

As he had done at Bern's, he didn't consult the menu but merely glanced at her for permission and then ordered for the two of them.

"All right," he said, resting his hands on the tabletop. "Ready when you are."

A relatively seasoned interviewer for her tender twenty-three years, Jenna experienced a bad case of flutters and had to resort to her prepared list of questions.

She didn't need reminding that those aquamarine eyes, so cool and indifferent now, had watched her "rise like Venus" out of the Tyrells' swimming pool only the night before. Involuntarily, she recalled the waves of desire that had broken over her when his handsome mouth had tugged with such delicious insistence at her breast.

"What's the first memory you have of your father?" she asked.

There was a palpable hesitation. "No comment," he said. "Off the record, that would deal with the time he came to Asheville to get me when I was eight. You probably know the story by now. But I don't intend to talk about it."

She remembered he was an attorney and probably immune to verbal fire.

"Back on the record," she said, "I'd like to hear *some* childhood impressions of him, if you'd be willing to share them. How did he seem to you . . . when you were eight?"

"Big," said Duke. "Like the master of all he surveyed. He seemed like a very powerful man."

"How did that power make you feel?"

"No special way. You just asked how he seemed to me."

"Well, was he a loving father? Did he pay a lot of attention to you?"

"I have no basis for comparison. But I never had any doubt that he loved me."

Her pencil was still poised above the paper, and she wrote down "powerful" and "master of all he surveyed," just to have something to do with her hands.

"When you came to the Bar-T," she asked, looking up, "did Ed T. do anything special to make you feel less alien, more a part of the family?"

"No comment." The lines of his strong, tanned features had arranged themselves into a forbidding look.

She hesitated, then backtracked. "You said he seemed powerful to you. Did you think then that you wanted to grow up to be like him?"

Duke gave his napkin and fork a push. "What do you think?" he asked finally. "I assure you that I accomplish whatever I set out to do. *Am* I another Ed T. Tyrell?"

"Your father thinks so," she said. "But he also believes you've got your mother's 'gentle streak.'"

Something perilously akin to anger flashed in Duke's eyes. "I'm going to tell you something right now, Jenna Martin," he said, "and I hope I won't have to repeat it. *Off the record,* you'll have to answer to me unless you keep my mother out of this article."

The waitress brought their barbecue sandwiches on platters heaped with French fries and pickle chips and deposited them in the midst of an emotionally charged silence. Duke had ordered coffee, black, with his meal. He shook his head when the waitress asked if they needed anything else.

"Well, y'all enjoy your meal, Mr. Tyrell," she said with a warm little smile as she hurried off to the next customer.

For a moment or two they busied themselves with their food, Duke's anger like a tangible presence between them. Then, the hot barbecue burning her mouth, Jenna swallowed a deep draught of her tea and tried again.

"I've gotten the impression your mother was the love of Ed T.'s life, that he loves her still," she ventured, half expecting him to upset the contents of the tabletop in her lap and storm out of the restaurant.

He did neither. *"Off the record,"* he said clearly and deliberately and furiously, "I'm not going to answer your damn questions. As far as you're concerned, Mary Courtenay did not exist."

Jenna didn't reply and he continued to stare at her, his face like stone.

"I'm sorry," she acknowledged finally. "Maybe I shouldn't have pressed you that way. I'm just trying to do my job."

"I don't give two cents for your job," he said in a tightly controlled voice.

"That's understandable. Please . . . eat your sandwich."

Looking as if he wished he'd never set eyes on her, he complied.

"Let's talk about the present," she said, hoping the tremor in her voice wasn't noticeable. She was aching to the bone with his displeasure, but determined not to lose total control of the interview. "That ought to be safe enough. On the record, what kind of relationship do you have with your father now?"

He swallowed a bite of his sandwich and washed it down with coffee. "We love and respect each other," he said.

She made a show of writing that down. "Could you be more specific?"

"If you'll ask a more specific question."

"I'm trying. Do the two of you work closely in business and family matters?"

"Yes, we do."

"He is still the active head of the family business?"

"Yes."

"Does he regard you as his heir apparent?"

There was an ominous pause.

"Off the record," he said, "you're not going to get me to say that. Even if it *is* true. Members of my family

cooperate with one another in business and I don't intend to needlessly offend anyone by shooting off my mouth. Or make things any tougher for Neddy than they already are."

When he mentioned Neddy, his deep voice became protective in the way she'd known it could. Jenna felt a certain surprise. I didn't think you even *liked* Neddy, she rejoined silently.

Then she realized he had managed to signal for the check without missing a beat of their antagonistic interchange. He was laying some folding money atop it now, probably including a generous tip.

"If you're almost finished," he said, "I've some lobbying to do at the courthouse before the commission sits this afternoon as the zoning board of appeals."

"I suppose you're back on the record with that remark," she said, attempting a smile.

"Sure." The corners of his mouth lifted slightly. "You can print it, if you want."

She pursed her lips a little, unaware of how pretty and unsure of herself she looked, sitting there in her businesslike suit with rosy cheeks and a sophisticated hairdo.

"I'd really appreciate it if you could give me another minute or two," she told him.

"All right."

By now, Jenna felt as if the interview was a total failure. But she had to have something to write on the lined, blank pages, if only to salvage her self-respect.

"Could you describe your father's personality by listing what you think are his essential traits?" she asked. "What qualities typify the man?"

Dutifully he considered the question, as if he regarded his answer to be a sort of ransom he must pay to escape the interview.

"It would be almost impossible to think of Ed T. in terms of abstract qualities," he said at last. "He's a complex man, and my father. There's an almost . . . mystical bond between us. I guess if I had to come up with a quick description of what he's like, I'd say he's witty and warm and clever. Sometimes difficult. Hard-nosed and sure of himself and very loving. Will that do?"

She had been scribbling furiously, covering the page with jagged script that would be difficult to decipher if she let the notes get too cold.

"Yes, that's what I was after," she said, realizing she would have exactly one paragraph of good material from the interview. "Thank you very much."

"Don't mention it."

Their eyes met and for a second she thought he had forgotten his anger and was remembering the intimate details of their previous night's adventure.

But all he said was, "I see you haven't finished your sandwich. I do have to get back across the street. Mind if I just leave you here?"

Jenna's head was aching. She tried to ignore what she considered an idiotic surge of disappointment. "Not at all," she managed. "I have to go over these notes anyway. See you later."

With a little gesture of deference, he left her, stopping to talk with several men and women friends before leaving the restaurant.

Her eye fell back to the page. Duke might have been talking about Ed T., she thought with a sudden tingle of awareness, but that description could be applied to him equally as well. Afraid she was falling in love with him, she sat quietly for a moment, surrounded by the bustle of the cafe, and just closed her eyes.

That afternoon, Jenna was scheduled to interview Neddy—by the pool, at his request. Jumping back into her rental car, she returned to the ranch with an hour to spare, went to her room, and lay down with a cold cloth on her throbbing temples.

Without meaning to, she fell asleep. She was awakened by a knock at her door. Opening it, she found Neddy lounging against the door frame, drink in hand as usual. He was clad in swimming trunks and a polo shirt.

"Have you forgotten our date?" he drawled. "You look like you've been sleeping in your clothes."

"Sorry," said Jenna, disliking the way she always seemed to end up apologizing to these Tyrells. "Just give me a moment to change."

"Sure," he said, not moving. "No problem."

"Mr. Tyrell . . ." she began, still half asleep and annoyed all out of proportion by his harmless leering.

"Neddy to you, Jenna Martin," he said.

"Neddy. Please wait for me on the terrace."

"Yes, ma'am. I'll even fix you a little drink."

"Make it iced tea," she called after him, shutting the door.

I wonder why I keep thinking of Neddy as younger than I when in fact he's six years older, she muttered, quickly discarding the wrinkled suit in favor of chino pants and a checked shirt.

Then suddenly the thought came to her that Neddy might have found her swimsuit top. Perhaps he was even planning to present it to her at poolside. I'll feel like I'm much his junior if that happens, she thought.

Unpinning her chignon and letting it fall into a single long braid at the back of her neck, she noted something she'd missed before—a small, brown-paper-wrapped package that had been placed unceremoniously by someone on one of the pink slipper chairs. Tearing off the wrapping, she withdrew the white crocheted bra that had caused so much embarrassment. A note, in a bold handwriting she recognized at once, fluttered to the floor.

It was from Duke.

"I beat Neddy to the punch," he had written. "In future, if I untie this damn thing, try to hang on to it. By the way, there's a pool where we don't need suits at all at Holly Hill." His scrawled signature was barely legible.

Jenna's cheeks burned with a mixture of ire and grudging admiration. In typically arrogant fashion, he had ordered her to keep better track of any of her garments he might occasionally care to remove.

He'd left little doubt that he considered her fair game and would mount another attack on her virtue. She felt her pulse quicken at the thought of swimming with him in the way he'd described in the pool on his estate. And though she was certain he'd left the package in the morning, before the hostile episode in the Crest Cafe, she had a feeling the little note was an open invitation, one that would still hold good.

Hastily, she thrust both note and suit top under her pillow. Then, snatching up her spiral pad and ballpoint, she hurried down the stairs to join Neddy Tyrell.

The interview went far better than she'd expected. Oh, there was no doubt of Neddy's curiosity about what had happened between herself and Duke the night before, and his jealousy of the vibrant man five years his senior was obvious. But, though he made a great show of disappointment when she appeared at poolside in her clothes instead of her swimming suit, Jenna felt he wasn't really jealous of her as a person.

No, she thought, as she settled in a lawn chair reluctantly holding a tall Bloody Mary with a fat celery stick, I can't count him a conquest. As preoccupied as he is with himself and his own problems, any reasonably present-able girl would do.

She guessed he would prefer a girl who'd attracted his uncle's attention. Yes, she repeated to herself, taking a wary sip of the fiery concoction he'd given her and setting her glass on the pool deck, he wants to take all he can away from Duke. Duke, she was certain, understood the situation all too well. His remark about not making things tougher for Neddy hovered in her mind.

With a sigh, she flipped open her notebook. "I understand you've lived with your grandfather most of your life," she said.

He nodded.

"Why is that? And what are your first memories of him?"

Neddy sipped at his drink, leering at her pleasantly. "I'll have to think about first memories a minute," he said. "I guess I told you my father, Yancey Tyrell, was the black sheep of this family. He and my mother, who was the despair of *her* parents, couldn't settle down.

"They split up when I was a year old and Ed T. insisted I come to live here. Grandma Elizabeth's nurse took care of me."

Jenna's head was buzzing with questions.

"Grandma Elizabeth was Ed T.'s wife, wasn't she? And paralyzed."

"Right on both counts."

"She was still alive when you came to the Bar-T?"

"My, yes. She died when Caroline was three." Neddy's brown eyes narrowed and the corners of his mouth turned up in a puckish smile. "You're wondering about where Duke's mother fits into the picture, aren't you?" he said.

Stabbed by guilt, as if she were betraying Duke, Jenna nodded.

"Well, I'll tell you. You see, Grandma Elizabeth wasn't much of a wife to Ed T.—hadn't been for years. She got her polio when my daddy was just a baby, and she spent her life in a wheelchair, tending all those plants you see on the sun porch and reading her Bible. She was a sweet lady, but I always used to think it was a relief to her not to have to keep up with him.

"Ed T., he had lots of women, but nobody to ease the heart, if you know what I mean. He was busy in the legislature a lot. But when Joe Courtenay hired on here and brought his pretty wife to live in the cottage the Nuñezes have now, something happened.

"The Courtenays didn't have any children, but there was one expected. Right after Mary Courtenay miscarried, old Joe decided to head up to Alaska and work a gold claim. And he didn't want a woman weighing him down."

He paused, sipped again at his drink, and watched her face. Keeping her professional composure, Jenna waited.

"Mary Courtenay stayed on here as a cook," he continued finally. "Now Ed T. and Duke are two of a kind. They see something they want and they go after it. Ed T. wanted Mary and he got her.

"Then, when Duke was on the way, Joe came back. He threatened to expose Ed T. and ruin his political career if she didn't go away with him. So she went.

"Later, when she died, Ed T. brought Duke back here to live. My daddy was in Hong Kong at the time and my mother on the Riviera, so I was here already."

Jenna shook her head. "How old were you then?"

"About two."

She winced, imagining how confused the small Neddy must have been, both hostile to and adoring of the older boy who had come between himself and his grandfather.

"Is . . . Caroline your half-sister then?" she asked.

"Nope. Mother and Daddy got together again long enough to produce her before they were killed in a car accident."

"So she never knew your parents?"

"No more than I did."

"I guess Ed T. was really like a father to you."

He shrugged and gave an ironic smile that tore at her heart.

"Not really. Duke is his *son,* and the only child of the woman he loved. My daddy was a disappointment to him. He doesn't let anyone forget that."

Jenna drew in her breath softly. "I wouldn't blame you if you felt some resentment," she said .

"Of Duke?" He arched one eyebrow at her, that crooked grin of his widening a bit. "Sure, I resent him. He's everything I'll never be. But I have to admire the b——"

Stopping before he said the word, he laughed outright and got to his feet to replenish his empty glass from the portable bar.

"There *is* that additional problem," he confided. "Y'all have to watch your language when you've got a child born on the wrong side of the blanket in the driver's seat." The half-serious little joke with its mixed metaphor failed to hide the truth of how tough things really were for Neddy.

6

That night Jenna and Ed T. talked until nearly eleven. Again he told stories of how his father, Judge Tyrell, had required his three sons, Ed, Burton—who was now deceased—and Everett, to work like ranch hands and grove pickers as they learned the business.

Yancey had not done that—in accord with his mother's wishes, Ed T. added. But Duke had been raised exactly like a Tyrell. Despite his college degrees, he could do any job that needed doing on the ranch.

As they talked, the questions drifted to Ed T.'s political life, how he'd gotten started in politics, the deals he had made and the people he'd known. Surprised at his frankness, Jenna asked why he was being so open with her.

"At my age, honey," he said, "you're as safe as you'll ever be. People tend to indulge you if you want to brag about your sins."

Duke did not put in an appearance that night. The next morning she left early for Tampa to interview Aunt Bliss and have lunch with her friend Beth Kidder, a former classmate at Northwestern who now worked a courts beat for the Tampa *Tribune*. They planned to share a few days' vacation when her assignment was complete.

Aunt Bliss's house on Ballast Point Way was set back behind an iron grillwork fence and tall hedges of bougainvillea and oleander. Of white brick, and two stories tall with a pillared veranda and shutters in a soft rose color, the old home was gracious to the point of gentility. Beyond it was the hazy blue of Hillsborough Bay.

Azaleas like flames in every shade of pink and red imaginable banked the circular brick drive. Jenna half expected a servant in formal morning coat to open her car door and hand her a mint julep.

The tall front door with its lovely leaded glass fanlight was opened by a black woman of indeterminate age who wore a neat gray dress with white collar and cuffs.

"Miss Bliss is out back, doin' her roses," said the woman, who introduced herself with a smile as Thalia Jones. "This way, please."

They traversed the breezy quarry-tiled central hall, passing gracefully curving stairs on their way to the rear French doors. Jenna glimpsed a dining room with delicate old mahogany furniture and a crystal chandelier, a book-lined study, a pantry with glass-paneled cream wooden cupboards.

Bliss Sanford, despite her fragile age of seventy-six, was on her knees in cotton pants and shirt in the rose bed, dusting and pruning her prize roses. Dark glasses and a straw hat hid her face. Her hands with their enormous diamond rings were encased in cotton gardening gloves. There was a smudge of garden dirt on her cheek.

Beyond her, the lawns of her estate stretched green and well cared for under the oaks and Sabal palms toward the seawall and boathouse.

"Well, my dear, you must pardon me," she said with a smile, getting to her feet with Thalia Jones's help. Her brown eyes, so like Ed T.'s, appraised Jenna's bone-colored sharkskin suit, peach blouse, and neat hairdo.

"I'm badly dressed to entertain," she added. "But at my age people forgive me for it." Stripping off her gloves, she invited Jenna to join her at a green wrought-iron table that Thalia had arranged with much-washed everyday damask, Minton china, and fresh flowers.

Catching Jenna's return appraisal, she made an astute comment. "I suppose you're thinking," she said, "that I sound just like my brother. But the truth is, Tyrells at any age find excuses for doing exactly what they want to do."

Jenna laughed. "I'm sure that's right," she said, taking a seat across from her hostess. "You have a lovely home, Aunt Bliss."

"It's the Sanford place," replied Ed T.'s sister without hesitation. "When I go, it will belong to Hollings Sanford, my late husband's nephew."

"You didn't have any children of your own, did you?"

The old woman shook her head. "Just Hollings, and his two babies, Cole and Mary Lou. And of course Duke and Neddy and Caroline. By the way, how is your romance going with that boy?"

Jenna reddened. "I suppose you mean Duke," she said awkwardly.

Aunt Bliss chuckled. "The same."

"We're . . . not exactly having a romance. He got awfully angry yesterday when I asked him about his mother and how he came to the Bar-T to live."

"You *do* have spunk," said Aunt Bliss admiringly.

Meanwhile, Thalia Jones was dishing out blueberry and peach compote and creamed veal on biscuits and pouring coffee from a china pot.

"That's a touchy subject with him and always has been," Aunt Bliss added. "I'll tell you about Ed and Mary Courtenay, if you like. I even have a picture of her upstairs."

"I'd love to see it," Jenna said.

"Well, you shall." The old woman patted her hand.

Briefly, Jenna filled her in on that part of the story Neddy had already told her.

"All true," said Bliss Sanford. "But of course Neddy doesn't realize the extent of my brother's feeling for Mary.

"It was as if Ed wanted to ravage her and protect her at the same time, from the moment he laid eyes on her—even though she was carrying her husband's child just then. I couldn't blame him—he'd been lonely so long and she was such a pretty little thing, with those huge eyes the color of Duke's and that mass of auburn curls.

"And she was strong—not an apathetic clinging vine like Elizabeth or even a bystander like myself. She was one of those people who plunge into life, take risks. . . ."

Aunt Bliss was silent a moment, remembering.

"Ed T. fell in love with her at once," she said, taking up the thread of the story again. "But he tried not to let her know. Then, when Joe Courtenay left for Alaska, he made his move—bought the Holly Hill place for her and took her there."

Jenna was silent.

"I suppose he knew it was wrong to do that," Aunt Bliss continued, "that, in a way, he was hurting both Mary and Elizabeth. But he couldn't divorce an invalid—even if he *weren't* speaker of the Florida House. And he couldn't bear to let Mary go."

"If it weren't for the solution he chose," said Jenna softly, "there'd be no Duke. Anyone can see that Duke is the joy of his old age."

"Yes." The old woman swallowed a mouthful of veal and biscuit. "Duke is a delight—to Ed T. most certainly, *and* to me and Caroline. Even to Neddy and his cousins, I daresay, though they have mixed emotions."

"Tell me more about Mary."

"There's not much to tell. I went out to Holly Hill to see how she was about a week before Joe turned up again. She was seven months pregnant with Duke and I have never seen anyone more radiantly happy than she was. She positively glowed with contentment."

She paused. "Mary Courtenay loved my brother with all her heart," she said, "and it was with the greatest pleasure that she carried his child. I agree with Neddy that she left Ed T. only to save him from ruin, and I'd venture to add that she went on loving him the rest of her life, with no regrets."

"The way he loved her?"

"My, yes. He searched the country for her after she just vanished that terrible day. I think he'd have given up everything he had to get her back, and their baby. But the only letter he ever got from her was posted by their son after her death."

Jenna realized there were tears in her eyes. "It's a heartbreaking story," she said. "No wonder Duke doesn't want it told."

Aunt Bliss nodded. "Some of it will have to be told if you're going to do any real story on my brother's life," she said. "I think you respect Duke, so I leave it to your discretion how much you should tell."

The faded image of Mary Courtenay, wearing a housedress and voluminous apron and standing beside her husband Joe in a portrait of the ranch help, didn't tell Jenna very much. There was an impression of vitality, but she couldn't push the family resemblance to Duke beyond a certain faint likeness. He was too much his father's son.

With Aunt Bliss's permission, she slipped the photograph into a manila envelope to borrow it, then thanked her hostess and wished her good-bye.

"Tell Ed when you see him that I'm going to stay in town a while longer," was Bliss Sanford's parting comment. "I'll see you when the whole gang comes down here for my brother's birthday. You'll be able to get some good pictures then."

Jenna had spent several hours with Aunt Bliss and she was nearly twenty minutes late for her lunch date with her friend Beth. Switching over to Beth's car at the *Tribune,* they chatted without pause, catching up on each other's love lives and careers on their way to Friday's, the restaurant Beth had selected.

"I got somebody to cover for me this afternoon," said Beth as they walked into the greenery-swathed pub and found a table. "I've got all afternoon. It's a good thing you're late, because during the lunch hour this place . . ."

Beth's voice trailed off as her eyes widened a bit behind her glasses.

"Isn't that your current flame and antagonist just across the room?" she asked in surprise.

"Surely you don't mean Paul Linski . . ." Jenna began, turning a little to see.

It was Duke, seated at a table for two with a slim, elegant blonde about five years Jenna's senior. They were speaking intimately and he was holding her hand.

Jenna's face burned. "Who . . . is she?" she asked, not caring if Beth noted her chagrin.

"That's Mary Lou Davies, the wife of U.S. Representative Franklin Davies," said Beth promptly. "She's 'old Tampa.' Davies is one of Duke's law partners. And so is her father, Hollings Sanford."

Jenna stared. "She's . . . his cousin?" she asked.

"Well," said Beth, "sort of. By marriage, or a couple of times removed. I understand she's one of his old girl friends. They were an item before she married Davies a few years back."

Tight lipped, Jenna watched Duke and his lunch date for a moment and then tore her gaze away.

"How many old girl friends does he have, anyway?"

"Quite a few. Darn near every unattached female in the courthouse and a few who *are* attached are in love with him."

So am I, thought Jenna, feeling sick in the pit of her stomach. I don't want to be. But so am I. And I'm burning up with jealousy.

Mercifully, Duke didn't see her, and she kept her back turned to him for most of what turned out to be a miserable luncheon. Agreeing to whatever plans Beth suggested when she could concentrate sufficiently to learn what they were, she glanced back at Duke's table near the end of the meal.

He and Mary Lou Davies had gone.

"I hope you're over Duke Tyrell by the time we take our little trip," observed Beth pointedly but with a certain sympathy. "Or I might as well go alone."

"Believe me," said Jenna, gritting her teeth. "I'm going to work on it."

After lunch, Jenna insisted she and Beth go ahead with their intended shopping tour. With several packages in hand, she returned to the ranch at about four thirty and promptly bumped into Duke in the foyer.

"So," she said shortly, "you do come home sometimes."

"As a matter of fact . . ." He stopped, probably aware she had no intention of pausing to converse with him. "See you at supper," he called after her instead as she started up the stairs. "Hold down your appetite and we'll have a swim later."

She was thankful he couldn't see her face. "Sorry, I'm not in the mood," she retorted over her shoulder, going into her room and shutting the door.

Dinner was decidedly awkward, as far as Jenna was concerned. The company consisted of herself and three men—Duke, Ed T., and Neddy—who seemed bent on teasing her and paying her the maximum amount of attention.

Probably realizing that she would refuse to be alone with him again, Duke adroitly arranged a poker game to while away the evening. When Jenna protested that she didn't know how to play and was not much of a gambler, he wouldn't hear of her begging off.

"I'll teach you and stake you myself," he said with such a lively glint in his eyes that she couldn't refuse. "It'll be to your professional advantage, anyway. You can't really say you know the Tyrells until you've played our brand of poker."

After they finished their game, Duke walked her to the bottom of the stairs before going in to say good night to his father.

"How about riding out with me in the morning?" he

90

said. "You haven't seen the ranch, and Ed T. wants me to tell you a bit about the way the place operates, what our holdings are . . ."

"I . . . I'm not sure I should."

He frowned. "Don't you ride?"

"Oh, well of course."

"I see. You have my faithful promise I won't behave like I did in the Crest Cafe. I'll be my most gracious self."

He waited.

Darn him, thought Jenna. Must he always stand so close? She could smell his particular blend of tobacco and moss and sunburned skin and it was next to impossible not to remember the intimate moments they'd shared. Probably Mary Lou Davies has similar and very recent memories, she thought, steeling herself. How many women does he need?

"I'll be very grateful for a tour of the ranch and whatever information you care to give me," she told him at last, her voice distinctly cool. "What time do we depart?"

"After breakfast. About eight thirty or so."

Still he stood there, watching her as if he'd like to say something more.

"I forgot to thank you for returning my bikini top," she said, deliberately bringing up the incident in the swimming pool to show him she didn't care. "Even though, under the circumstances, it was the least you could do. Good night."

The following morning was a beautiful one, clear and breezy and cool. Overhead the sky was a blue dome and all around them green and brown pastures spread out as far as the eye could see. Duke courteously volunteered information in a way Jenna couldn't fault, though she wished he did not look quite so handsome and appealing in the saddle, with his erect bearing and rippling thigh muscles in the closely fitted blue jeans.

"We're lucky we don't have bog fires, it's been so dry this winter," Duke commented as they mounted a ridge crowned with a grapefruit grove about an hour out of the stables. Below they could see a flat pasture dotted by cattle and what Duke called "bay heads"—islands of cypress trees standing on their knobby roots in low, swampy areas. In the distance, rows of orderly green citrus trees marched over a swelling rise.

Their horses had stopped next to each other to graze as they surveyed the scene and she was startled when Duke reached out to cover her hand on the reins with one of his own.

"Jenna," he said, "tell me—why are you so mad at me? I thought we parted friends—almost—at the Crest. Is it because of the way I was fresh with you in the pool? Or the note I sent? I'd like to clear it up, because I want to be fresh with you again."

For a moment she choked, unable to reply. "Not exactly," she said finally, determining suddenly to tell him the truth. "I realize we don't owe each other anything. I just don't like it when you pursue me and a dozen other women at the same time. It makes me feel . . . cheap."

He was frowning in earnest now. "What in God's name do you mean?"

"I happened to be in Friday's last afternoon when you were there holding hands with Mary Lou Davies."

"And you think . . ." He broke off and laughed with surprised amusement. "Jenna, you little firebrand," he said. "You're jealous!"

"No, I'm not!" she exclaimed, wrenching her hand away so that her horse jerked back a little on the bit. "I wouldn't let myself care about someone like you."

"Wouldn't you?" His eyes had narrowed to slits of aquamarine fire. "Well, it might interest you to know that Mary Lou came to me with a personal problem. Her husband has been rampantly unfaithful and she wants a divorce. She isn't sure whom she should get for an attorney, with Franklin and her father in the same firm. It's going to be a mess for her, and she wanted my advice."

Jenna stared. "Five'll get you ten she's in love with you," she blurted.

He gave her a wicked smile. "Is that so hard for you to understand? Anyway, even if you're right, the feeling isn't mutual. Now, can we get down from these beasts so I can kiss you?"

With easy grace, he swung from the saddle and held out his hands to her. Half dazed by the crumbling of her angry illusions, she placed her palms on his shoulders.

A moment later she was on the ground with his arms about her. Hungrily, his mouth bruised hers, as demanding and intimate as it had been that night in the pool.

Looming powerfully over her, his back and shoulders were hers again to stroke, caress through his checked cotton shirt. Something went weak within her as she molded the hollows of her palms and the tips of her fingers to his broad muscles, then let her hands stray to the small of his back, his lean, narrow waist.

With all her heart she longed to reach lower still, to fit one hand to the muscled hardness of his lean masculine hips and pull him closer against her. Only reason kept her from doing as she wished.

"Jenna, Jenna," he murmured after some minutes, letting her breathe deeply at last, though he still imprisoned her. With a slight tremor, his hands moved to unpin her hair. "I can't leave you alone. Say you feel the same."

"Duke, please . . ."

"Tell me so," he demanded roughly, "if it's true."

Her eyes widened as his embrace tightened even more, so that she could feel all too clearly now the hard outline of his desire against her thigh.

"I . . . *can't leave you alone.*" To her astonishment, the confession he'd wrung from her made scarcely any sound.

"Darling Jenna," he said with barely restrained passion and yet the most indescribable tenderness. "I want to make love to you . . . right here on the ground, or anywhere you say. You make me *wild* . . . to plunge into you and take all of your sweetness, to fill you up . . . with the way I need you. Since the night we met, I haven't been able to think of anything else."

Her last hairpin had fallen and she shook free the weight of her hair, so that it cascaded around her shoulders.

Still she struggled. "No, Duke," she whispered. "I can't let you."

"Why not? Don't you think I'd be able to please?"

Agonized at his kisses on her throat, she could only imagine how much. What would you say, she asked him silently, if I told you it was because I could really care about you that I'm hesitating? Would you be all too quick to back away?

"My . . . assignment," she stammered. "I don't think we should . . ."

"We don't have to agree about that to make love." He paused, kissing her again. "*Will* you, Jenna?" he asked. "Will you let me become your lover?"

Tender and reasonable, his words broached her defenses. She felt herself sway a little as he pushed up her sweater and caressed her breasts, teasing her nipples to erect readiness for his marauding tongue.

She shut her eyes as he lowered his head to kiss them. Each new sensation seemed to engulf her more completely than the last, until she thought she would drown, there on the crest of the ridge, in her need for him.

"I have a blanket, sweetheart," he said thickly as he nuzzled her. "And a jacket you can roll up for your head. Say you'll let me love you."

The words to deny him wouldn't come, and he took her little moan of pleasure for assent.

He had spread the blanket on the ground and was

getting out his jacket when they heard the rattling sound, paralyzingly close to her ankles.

"Don't move." The words, terse with a fear that was close to panic, came from Duke. She froze.

He laid one finger on his lips. The rattling, like dry gourds or dice held in a cup, continued, making cold sweat stand out on Jenna's upper lip. Slowly, ever so slowly, Duke was reaching for the pistol she'd seen in his saddlebag, lifting it out, taking aim.

There was a sharp report as the gun blazed and a skittering sound in the dust beside her. Though her lungs tore with a silent scream, she stood rooted to the spot as if she were made of stone. Only her eyes ventured to dart sideways and down to rest on the diamondback rattler, now partially uncoiled. It was dead. She could feel her knees start to buckle.

"Sweetheart, you're trembling!" he exclaimed, the gun dropping from his hand as he enfolded her in his arms. "To think what could have happened! Say you're all right."

How strong he felt, how safe! If only she could always rest here, in his protection. Letting herself shake now, she relaxed against him with a little moan, her face pillowed against his shirt.

"I will be, Duke," she managed. "Thanks to you."

He continued to hold her, his hand rubbing her back comfortingly under the sweater. His other hand smoothed down her mane of hair like a pelt.

"I ought to be shot," he said, "for putting you in such danger."

"No, no," she whispered. "Don't blame yourself. You couldn't know."

They were silent a moment. "We'll have to go back down," he said finally, his voice full of regret. "They'll have heard the shot and somebody will be up here before long."

Kicking the rattler aside, he picked up his gun and the

blanket and helped her back into the saddle. Her sweater still rode higher than it should have on her ribs and he reached up to smooth it into place.

Their eyes met, and it came to her with force what had almost happened. She and this tall, pantherlike man with aquamarine eyes and arrogant, irreverent ways had very nearly joined their bodies together. After their encounter in the swimming pool, she could make an educated guess at what an exquisite pleasure that would have been.

She could feel her face flush even as she shivered a little.

"Sure you're all right?" he asked.

When she nodded, he mounted his stallion and then turned to her. It seemed the same thought had been in his mind.

"You would have let me take you," he said quietly, making a statement of it.

A vivid image of the two of them on the blanket came to her mind, causing the truth to burst from her lips. "Yes," she admitted breathlessly. "I suppose you're right."

His eyes held hers as if trying to read her very thoughts. "I still intend to have you, Jenna," he told her at last. "Though to do it I won't put you in harm's way again."

7

Ed T. was at the stables in his golf cart, driven there by a ranch hand when the news of the gunshot was radioed in. He was all concern extracting the story of what had happened from her while Duke went into the house to take a long-distance phone call.

When she could, she excused herself, declining lunch and stating that she wanted nothing more than a bath, a nap, and the chance to work undisturbed that afternoon in her room. Desperately, she needed time alone, to think, to sort out her feelings.

Stripping off sweater and pants, she showered thoroughly. Then, putting on a cotton Japanese wrapper her father had brought her years before from San Francisco, she settled on the pink chaise lounge by the window.

There was a knock on her door. Probably Ed T. had insisted something be sent up.

"Yes," she called.

When she opened the door, Duke stepped inside and closed it again. Then he took her in his arms.

"Not here!" she choked under her breath.

He laughed softly, for a moment very like his father. "Give me *some* credit, sweetheart," he said. "I trust there aren't any rattlesnakes in your bedroom. But in any case, I don't want us to be interrupted again."

His presence was having its familiar effect on her. She could feel her defenses weaken, and when he put his hand inside the front of her Japanese wrap, she didn't protest.

"Your breasts are so soft," he said into her ear as he kneaded them gently. "Touching them makes fire run through my veins. And it makes me want to reconsider your little bed."

Unable to stop herself, she glanced at the bed, saw in her mind's eye the two of them lying entwined there. To have him in that way . . .

Outside her door there were footsteps, approaching and then receding. One of the maids. Or Neddy again.

"Please," she begged. "Someone is sure to hear us."

"Not if you'll be quiet." He lowered his mouth to one breast and kissed it softly, pushing lazily at it with his tongue as if he had set aside the rest of the day to make love to her.

To Jenna's dismay, her body seemed to have a will of its own and it arched shamelessly against him, boldly confessing her need and making a sham of any contrary pretense.

"I . . . can't let you here," she whispered.

He tightened his embrace, as if the conflicting emotions she felt only made her that much more desirable.

"Your hair is damp at the back of your neck," he observed in that deep, faintly accented voice that could turn her knees to water. "You feel so vulnerable."

She couldn't reply. But she realized he was holding her now protectively, as he had for several moments in the pool that night, and on the ridge after the snake had threatened her.

"I have other plans for us than a few stolen moments making love to each other within earshot of my family," he said. "But that's not what I came to tell you. I have to go to Tallahassee for several days on business. But when I get back, I intend to take up exactly where we left off."

For a moment, her usually spirited nature came to the fore.

"I'm not promiscuous," she told him heatedly.

But he was not to be dissuaded. "That only makes you

more delectable, sweetheart," he said, bringing his mouth down on hers to probe it sweetly with his tongue.

One hand squeezed her waist through the thin cotton fabric. Deep in her woman's body, he evoked a curious, pleasantly painful emptiness that only what he was suggesting would assuage.

Much more of this, she thought, her cheeks flushed as if with a fever, and I'll be urging him across the room and drawing back the coverlet, not fending him off.

Then a thought struck her. Was it possible, she wondered, that he might feel more than casual attraction for her? Might he not want her in the same way that she wanted him? His next words gave her just a glimmer of hope.

"At least say you're willing to date me when I get back," he said, his eyes compelling. "Acknowledge to the world that we're very friendly enemies. I should be back by Friday, and I want to take you to hear the Guarnieri Quartet."

She knew him well enough now not to be amazed at his educated taste or the way he could enjoy everything from country music to one of the world's most renowned groups of classical string musicians. But it gave her an absurd pleasure to think that he would publicly admit his attraction for her, take to his bosom an upstart Yankee writer who was opposing his wishes simply because he could not do without her.

"I . . . I'd be delighted, Duke," she said.

"And you won't shy away from being called my girl?"

The question probed a tender point. Probably his father had told him of her denial of that very label.

"No," she conceded, "if that's what I am to be."

"It *is*. With all rights and privileges that pertain thereto." He kissed her again, as if to set a seal on their bargain. "Haven't you known from the beginning that's what would happen?" She could only nod affirmatively, chagrined at the way he must always wrest the truth from her. "Don't fall into anyone else's snare while I'm away."

Just brushing her lips with his own this time and giving her a little squeeze, he left her.

That goes double for you, Duke Tyrell. She sent the silent message after him as she closed the door. Wherever you go, she added, there must be legions of women just waiting to be taken into your arms.

She had agreed to be "Duke's girl," something she'd vowed not to do. She would now become one in a long line of women on whom he'd focused his attention, the current *amour* he burned to possess. Yet, though reason told her she was unlikely to be the last, something about the reasonable, loving way he had put his request seemed to hint otherwise. She could almost believe that their relationship might be a lasting one.

During the next four days Jenna did some traveling of her own, making several trips to Tampa and a journey up to Gainesville to meet with former colleagues of Ed T.'s. Through these added interviews, she was able to flesh out the character of her subject, and she knew that, though the old man had done some unethical and self-serving things in his long career, he had been almost as much of a statesman as a politician. Always he had been flamboyant, bold, a taker from life with both hands, though his gentle side and concern for others had usually been apparent, too.

Like Duke, she thought, finding herself irresistibly attracted to that lust for life she found in both of them—a lust that was not diminished by the masterful control of it they shared.

Returning from Tampa on Friday morning, she gave way to the inevitable and stopped at a dress shop she and Beth Kidder had visited earlier. Without even trying on the dress that had caught her eye again, she bought it—a dress that would tell Duke in no uncertain terms how she felt about being his girl.

Constructed of a deep purple-blue silk gauze shot through with metallic gold thread and silky strands of azure and rose, it had a vee neckline that plunged to the waist, giving the lie to the modest though transparent long sleeves. The skirt, just brushing her ankles, would make her appear taller, more a match for him. She paid for it—an outrageous sum—with just a faint flush on her cheeks to give away her thoughts of what a pleasure it would be for Duke to remove it.

Duke had flown to Tallahassee but, to her annoyance, he returned to the ranch in the Howards' Lincoln. She had been in the barn chatting with Wayne Keeper when he arrived. So it wasn't until she was strolling back to the house, dressed casually in jeans and an old yellow sweater with several snags in it, her hair tied back in a ponytail that reached below her waist, that she caught sight of him getting out of the car.

Duke had been driving, she saw, with Vicki at his side while Pete Howard lounged in the back seat. Vicki was wearing an ivory raw-silk suit and a fuchsia shantung blouse that made her mahogany curls glow. She tossed her head provocatively at Duke, taking possession of his arm.

Though she felt shabby by comparison and about twelve years old beside the sophisticated Vicki, Jenna had no choice but to step forward to greet them. I wonder if Duke will shy away from me now, she thought. Maybe he's changed his mind about wanting me to be his girl.

Pete Howard met her tentative smile with a warm grin that was in direct contrast to his sister's cool expression. Vicki's hostile green gaze flicked insultingly over Jenna's childish hairdo, her informal clothing.

Let Vicki's looks kill, Jenna thought exultantly. Something in her soared as Duke shook off Vicki's arm without being too obvious and came over to her to take one of her hands in both his own.

"Any snares?" he inquired softly, lowering his voice so the others couldn't hear.

Trembling at the way even his casual touch could make

her feel now, she met his beautiful eyes. "None but yours," she replied.

He put one arm around her and turned to face his friends.

"I neglected to mention that I'd already asked Jenna to attend the Guarnieri performance with me this evening," he said in that cool way he had sometimes. "But I wouldn't be averse to making it a foursome, if she doesn't mind."

Mind? she thought furiously. I could kick you, Duke Tyrell, for even suggesting an evening with Vicki Howard.

"Why, of course I don't mind," she replied sweetly, even as she stiffened in his half-embrace.

He tightened his fingers on her waist. "It's settled then," he said, ignoring Vicki's surprise and anger. He nodded at her and her brother. "Y'all come on in and freshen up, have a drink," he said. "We don't have to leave for quite a while yet."

Irritated, Jenna pulled away from him a little as they went into the house. Immediately she felt his breath, warm on her ear.

"No need to get mad, sweetheart," he reassured her in a quiet undertone. "We'll be taking separate cars, and we'll definitely be ending the evening alone. You'll have me all to yourself. I promise."

The look she shot him contained a mixture of ire and embarrassment and pleasure.

He grinned at her, as wicked and handsome as ever, and certainly no more modest. "Now that we've got that settled," he whispered, "come on into Ed T.'s study and be gracious while I fix some drinks for my guests."

"I see the twist of lemon doesn't come just with Tyrell apologies," she retorted, suddenly joining into the spirit of his bantering. "It comes with Tyrell promises, too."

It had been the right thing to say. His grin broadened as she went to sit by Ed T. on the sofa, neatly preempting the seat Vicki would have chosen to emphasize her status as longtime friend of the family.

Ringing for the liquor cart to be brought in, Duke capably mixed drinks for all of them while Vicki and Pete drew up chairs. He fixed a vodka martini for Jenna and, despite her protests that she shouldn't be drinking on an empty stomach, he would not let her demur.

The Howards' drinks distributed and his own Scotch on the rocks in hand, he gave Ed T. his toothache medicine and sat beside Jenna, the hard muscular length of his thigh in the tailored brown trousers pressing against her own. As they talked, he slipped one arm casually across the sofa back behind her in a way that caused Pete and Ed T. to eye him speculatively and Vicki to fume.

Well, thought Jenna, liking the feel of him next to her and the way their contact discomfited her rival, if I'm to be Duke's girl, I might as well enjoy it to the utmost. And with that decision, she took a sip of the strange-tasting drink he'd made her and she joined into the conversation with genuine zest. Nor did she evince any surprise or awkwardness when Duke asked his father pleasantly how the interviews had been going.

"Fine, just fine," said the old man with a twinkle in his eye. "But our young friend here has spent a good bit of time this week gallivanting around the state, flirting with old cronies of mine. I'm getting jealous."

Duke was about to reply when Vicki interrupted sharply. "I thought you were irrevocably opposed to the story," she said with a side glance at Jenna. "Now you sound like you've accepted it. I didn't think you could be swayed so easily."

"I can't." His hand, holding his drink, just brushed against Jenna's knee, warning her to be quiet. "I'm still opposed to it," he added. "But Ed T. is boss around here and he wants the article written. Jenna and I . . . don't find our differences about the story any barrier to friendship."

Vicki muttered something unintelligible and sipped angrily at her drink while Pete looked from Jenna to

Duke and back again. She could feel Ed T.'s warm but quizzical regard.

Wow! she thought, a little breathless at Duke's directness. He really meant it when he said we'd go public with our feelings for each other. I'm going to be in for a lot of ribbing and commentary now.

Mercifully, Pete Howard introduced another topic and the conversation veered away from their romantic entanglement. After a while, it was time to go upstairs to dress.

Half an hour later, bathed, scented, and powdered, she took the beautiful gown from its hanger and slipped it over her head. It was without doubt the loveliest thing she had ever owned. And she would be wearing it for the man she loved.

Yes, I admit it, she said softly to herself as she viewed in the mirror her wide eyes, sleek hair, slender yet curving body half revealed, half concealed by the glittering diaphanous silk. I love him so much I could die of it. And I want him the same way. I want to give him everything I have.

Half wild with the notion, she strapped on gold kid sandals and picked up her cashmere wrap, in case he had the top down. He was waiting at the bottom of the stairs, exactly where Neddy had stood that first evening. She could feel his eyes, as warm as a touch, run along the swell of her cleavage before they returned to her own.

"My God, you're absolutely beautiful," he said solemnly, with no twist of lemon at all.

"Thank you," she said, taking his hand. "I'm glad I pass muster."

"Oh, you'll pass, believe me, sweetheart." The words were almost fierce, quite as if he did not want to share his vision of her at that moment with anyone.

Then he shrugged, led her back to the study where Pete and Vicki were waiting. She could feel the auburn beauty's jealousy like a lash. Gowned in a ravishing copper silk dress that did not plunge as low as Jenna's,

Vicki still managed to look worldly wise in a way that was not altogether charming.

Duke brought the Mercedes to the door himself. "See you at the Tampa Theatre," he told his friends, stowing her inside and taking off down the long drive before the others were even settled inside the Lincoln.

"I couldn't just dump my friends," he said shortly, turning onto the highway with a spray of gravel.

"I know."

"Then what are you doing over there? I thought you were my girl."

"I'm not over there now," she replied reasonably, coming into the circle of his arm.

Reaching down momentarily to kiss her, he drew her tightly against him, his fingers caressing her through the gauzy silk, taking every bit as much tactile pleasure in the sensuous material as she had known he would. Meanwhile she was half reeling with the scent and feel of him.

"You know, don't you," he asked, his deep voice full of emotion, "that I wanted to take you to Holly Hill tonight?"

The thought of them loving and sleeping together in a high old four-poster the way she had imagined it left her undone.

"Yes," she said, her admission breathless.

He slipped his hand into the front of her gown. "With the damn dinner they're taking us to afterward, it's going to be very late." He paused. "Will you come to my apartment instead?"

"Your . . . apartment?" She almost stammered it.

"I have a condominium on the bay, near Westshore."

Jenna didn't reply, hiding her face against his velvet dinner jacket, but both of them knew what her answer must be.

The Tampa Theatre, where the Guarnieri performed, was like a combination Moorish palace and cave frosted with stalagtites. Twisting columns, ornately carved plas-

ter, and elaborately painted decorations all added to the
exotic atmosphere. She sat between Duke and Pete
Howard, with Vicki on Pete's far side, listening with
heightened appreciation to chamber music by Beethoven
and Schubert and Mozart as it was interpreted by these
masters.

Later, at a glittering and elegant reception atop the
Exchange Bank, she let Duke ply her with champagne
and point out landmarks from the huge bank of windows
that overlooked the Hillsborough River and the lights of
the city. Introduced to the musicians, she spoke to them
freely—perhaps a little too freely. She suspected that the
champagne had loosened her tongue. By contrast, Vicki
Howard was growing more and more morose as the
evening progressed.

Then, when the dinner party broke up, Vicki seemed
to come back to life, almost as if she knew what was in
the wind. Volubly, she insisted on prolonging the evening, cajoling them into going dancing at a small cabaret
nearby.

At the cabaret, with a smoothness born of practice,
Vicki managed to maneuver Duke into being her partner,
leaving Jenna to step out onto the small dance floor with
Pete Howard. But, his duty done, Duke reclaimed her
almost immediately. He held her tightly in his arms,
scarcely moving to the music.

"You're such a fragrant, delicious armful," he whispered, placing soft little kisses on her neck in complete
disregard of who might see them. "I'm not going to be
able to wait much longer. Say you want me too."

The admission came much more easily this time.

"You know I want you."

"I like to hear you say it."

In reply she stumbled a little against him.

"Too much champagne?" he asked indulgently.

"I . . . don't know. I'm not used to it." She giggled
softly. "Probably so," she added. "I feel so strange and
floaty . . ."

His arms tightened momentarily. "We're getting out of here," he said, "Victoria Howard be damned."

They made their good-byes abruptly, Jenna forming her own words very carefully because suddenly she didn't trust her speech. The champagne had gone quite powerfully to her head, she realized.

From the Exchange it was but a short run in Duke's powerful car to the steel and glass building that housed his apartment. With courtesy and some amusement, he helped her out of the car and guided her into the elevator.

"You're actually tipsy, you know," he commented as he fitted his key into the apartment door. "And I love the way you carry it off, with such charming innocence. Thank goodness you already have some experience in lovemaking."

"Not very much," she blurted out, prodded to honesty by the champagne's effect.

They were just inside his door. He stood very close, all vibrant male animal. "What do you mean?" he asked. "You've always been so passionate and responsive when I touch you."

Jenna felt as if she would drown in his eyes. "I've had only one other lover," she said. "And, even in bed, he never made me feel what you do."

With something like a groan, he swept her up into his arms, carried her through a doorway into his bedroom, and switched on a soft lamp. His bed, spread with a silky dark blue quilt, was enormous. Despite her befuddled state, she recognized the artist whose work hung above it.

"Joseph Raffaele," she said, realizing that Duke's taste in art matched hers exactly as she took in the huge canvas of iridescent, multihued river stones covered with a transparent veil of gently flowing water. "There's one in the Art Institute . . ."

"Jenna." He set her on her feet, still keeping his arms about her and almost certainly noting her dizziness.

"Yes?" She slipped her arms around him, cradling him

close against her as she thought how much she loved him.

"Are you sure this is what you want? When . . . *if* you go back to Chicago, you won't be sorry?"

Oh, I'll be sorry, she thought, sorry it couldn't last forever. But I'll have him while I can.

"It's what I want, Duke," she whispered. "I only wish you could have been the first."

"As far as I'm concerned, there's never been anybody else for either of us," he responded, his voice rough with desire.

With a slight tremor in his hands that betrayed the depth of his feeling, he removed her hairpins, one by one, and unwound the heavy silken coils of hair that dropped to her shoulders.

"I could get lost in you," he murmured, his arms tightening about her as his kisses trailed from her mouth to the pulse at the base of her throat and then down the open front of her dress to her waist.

At the same time, he was expertly pulling down her zipper and the dress fell in a spangled, translucent cloud to the floor. The flesh-colored camisole followed, revealing her upturned breasts. Her bare arms and shoulders gleamed in the lamplight.

"My precious girl," he said, his gaze moving over her heated skin like a caress. "Do you know how exquisite you are?"

Jenna shook her head slowly.

Not I, she replied, the words making no sound as she wove her fingers into the dark hair at the nape of his neck. *You're* the beautiful one.

Her senses reeled from the champagne and the passionate invitation that seemed to exude from his every pore. She was mesmerized by the latent power of his broad shoulders under the black velvet dinner jacket.

Give no quarter, she told him silently. Don't leave one inch of me untouched.

"Well, take my word for it, you are," Duke was saying as he smoothed back the curtain of hair and ran his fingers lightly over one breast.

A fresh wave of desire swept through her at his touch. Curling his hand around one hip, he drew her to the bed and turned back the quilted dark blue spread to reveal matching percale sheets in a wave pattern that dipped and swirled like crashing surf.

Her knees suddenly weak at the thought of what was happening, she sat down. He bent to remove her gold kid sandals, then straightened to take off his jacket and bow tie, the white dress shirt that only emphasized his maleness.

Lying back against his pillows and looking up at him, Jenna thought again what a truly beautiful man he was. She loved his sensuous yet gentle touch, the way his aquamarine eyes had gone smoky and narrow in the lamplight. Her gaze rested lingeringly on muscles rippling under tanned skin, on the silken mat of dark chest hair that tapered toward his loosened belt.

Oh, she thought, longing to stretch out her arms and enfold him. He's all I could ever want.

But she felt so dizzy from that champagne. She must have voiced the latter sentiment aloud.

"How much did you have, anyway?" he said, frowning.

"I . . . lost count." She held out her arms.

But something had changed in his face. "Wait a moment," he said.

To her surprise, he went to rummage in the closet, withdrawing a soft old blue workshirt with partially rolled up sleeves. "Here," he said, helping her to sit up a little. "You can use this for a nightgown."

"But . . . Duke. . . ."

He was fitting her hands into the sleeves. "You don't think I'd let our first time together be like this, do you?" he asked roughly, as if he were only just managing to keep his emotions in check. "When we finally make love, you're going to be fully aware of what's happening, not anesthetized by alcohol."

"You mean . . . *you just want me to go to sleep?*"

"That's right," said Duke. "With my arms around you."

Taking off his belt completely and doffing his trousers, he got into bed beside her in just his shorts, pulled the blanket over the two of them, and turned out the light. He brushed aside the tears on her cheeks, opening the unbuttoned blue shirt wider so that her breasts touched his chest.

"Jenna, Jenna," he said, his voice betraying both emotional strain and the very deepest tenderness. "Please don't cry. I'm not going to let you get away. Now, darling, let's just go to sleep."

8

Incredibly, she had done as he suggested—cuddled there in his arms. She had slept comfortably, deeply, despite his unfamiliar presence.

Now she awoke, her eyes teased open by the strong sunlight. The bright Florida sun edged into the room despite heavy cream-colored drapes drawn to cover what was probably a sliding glass door to a balcony.

Duke was no longer beside her. She had the feeling he had risen only minutes before. The pillow was still creased where his head had lain, and she could hear the sound of the shower being turned on, a glass shower door closing.

With some curiosity, she let her gaze travel about the room, taking in the ivory walls, the thick dark blue carpeting, the heavy honey-toned teak furniture, a woven wall hanging that looked as if it had come from South America. Overhead was the Raffaele work she remembered. Hooked over the edge of the closet door on a wooden hanger was her beautiful gown. Duke must have hung it up so that the creases would fall out. It will be horribly embarrassing, she thought, if I have to wear it back to the ranch.

Suddenly, she realized that the blue shirt she was wearing hung wide open, revealing her breasts and the curve of waist and stomach above her flesh-colored bikini panties. Her hair was spread out on the pillow in a disheveled tangle.

I must have presented the picture of abandonment to

111

him when he woke, she said to herself, quickly buttoning several buttons and knotting the shirttails at her waist. Now that she was fully awake, regrets came flooding back and she felt keenly her foolishness in drinking so much champagne. She felt a very personal guilt that their lovemaking had been canceled for her sake.

Will he want me now? she wondered as she heard the shower go off. Will the masterful Duke Tyrell, known to be an expert heartbreaker, bother again with a somewhat inexperienced, occasionally shy young woman fool enough to get tipsy when he wants to make love to her?

Jenna was sitting up hugging her knees when Duke emerged from the bathroom wearing a dark blue towel wrapped sarong style around his narrow hips. I've never seen a more masculine physique, *never*, she thought, even while she struggled with her guilt pangs and regrets.

"Good morning," he said soberly, not even a ghost of a smile lifting the corners of his mouth. "Any the worse for wear?"

"No," she said, and then added before she could stop herself, "I wish I were."

"Sweetheart," he said, "that's not what I meant."

Coming to sit beside her, he took her in his arms.

"I feel like such a fool," she said against his still damp chest hair. "I . . . really wanted . . ."

"Hush," he said. "I know. You were like a little kitten curled up against me last night—yet one with such an enticing, womanly shape."

He reached down to tuck the towel more firmly about him.

"Jenna," he continued, "I've been thinking. You're very different from any woman I've known, and I want things to be right for us. I . . . think we should wait until you complete your story, so there won't be any unfinished business between us. I want . . . to see how you'll feel about making love to me then."

Instinctively, she gave a little cry of protest. Did he

think she was just *using* him? "I'll feel exactly the same," she told him emphatically.

Lightly he placed a kiss on her mouth. "Let's hope so, sweetheart," he said softly. "Because I guarantee I will."

Her mouth set stubbornly, but she still looked more vulnerable than she knew. *"I don't want to wait."*

"Well," said Duke, "that makes two of us. The shower is all yours if you want it. And, since I'm going to drop this towel and start getting dressed in about thirty seconds, you might want to hustle on in." The wicked glint returned to his eyes as he spoke and she scurried with unseemly haste toward the shower.

Why didn't I just sit there and watch him? she wondered to herself as the water streamed down. That's what I really wanted to do. After all, it wouldn't be the first time I've seen a nude man.

But she knew the reason she had avoided that pleasure. Indulging her curiosity would have made the wait he was forcing on them even harder to bear.

When she came out, wrapped in a huge terry bath sheet he'd left for her and holding the shirt and lace panties, she saw with gratitude that Duke had found some deck pants that would probably fit her.

I wonder whose they are, she thought, taking them in with a sidelong glance.

"Caroline's," he said, as if she'd asked the question aloud. "She and some friends used the apartment last month. Now, back to the bathroom with you. I don't want my resolve tested until after I've had my coffee."

At the ranch all was in a bustle with Caroline home again to direct preparations for her grandfather's eightieth birthday party. No one commented on Jenna's get-up or the fact that she had stayed overnight in Tampa.

She did get some speculative looks, particularly from Wayne Keeper, Mrs. Haskins, and Caroline. Neddy had come in late and stayed abed late, so he wasn't yet aware of the state of things. Ed T.'s brown eyes sparkled with approval.

Let them think what they want, she decided with bravado. If I'd had my way, they'd be right.

From Caroline she was amazed to learn there would be an estimated two hundred guests at Ed T.'s birthday party, not including several reporters and cameramen from local newspapers and television stations. Countermanding a lifelong policy, Ed T. had agreed to allow the press to be briefly present for the cake-cutting ceremony.

"They tell me I'm an institution," he chuckled. "And so I guess I'll have to oblige them."

Three days before they were to depart for Aunt Bliss's house on Ballast Point, Jenna got what she was sure would be her best photo of Duke and his father. She had been taking pictures all along and by then everyone had gotten used to the whir of her motor drive.

Camera in hand, she had entered the study softly to catch the two of them standing almost in silhouette before the strong afternoon sunlight that was streaming in the west-facing bank of windows. They were talking quietly together: the old man, once tall, leaning on his cane; the big vibrant son, inclining protectively toward his father, gesturing to make a point.

Love and an understanding deeper than the words they were exchanging were etched indelibly in every line of the little scene. Loath to disturb them, yet realizing what kind of a shot it would be, she aimed and clicked away three times in rapid succession. The two men she had come to love turned to her.

"Come on in, Jenna sweetheart," said Ed T. with genuine welcome.

"I have a feeling that was a good one," Duke added quietly. "Sit down and I'll fix us all a drink."

When they departed for Tampa later in the week, they took with them a veritable retinue: Wayne Keeper, Mrs. Haskins, and even Rosalia Nuñez to help Thalia Jones and Aunt Bliss's yard man, Tomás.

By the morning of Ed T.'s birthday, all was in readiness. The family, including Jenna and Everett Tyrell, a younger and slightly heavier version of Ed T., joined the old man for breakfast on the terrace and presented their gifts.

From Caroline there was a new silver-headed cane; from Aunt Bliss, a lovely heather-toned sweater she had knitted herself; from Neddy, a case of very expensive Scotch. With a smile, Everett handed over some stock certificates his brother had been wheedling him to sell.

Duke's gift was an automatic video-taping device that could be set to store TV shows his father might otherwise miss. It included a tape player, Duke explained, and the tapes of a number of old movie favorites that could be shown on his television screen.

Ed T.'s delight in his new toy was obvious. "This boy of mine knows just how much I love gadgets," he exclaimed warmly, quite oblivious to Neddy's longing for an equal word of praise.

The old man came last to Jenna's present—a flat rectangular package. But when he opened it, tears were bright in his eyes, and he clumsily wiped away one that strayed down his soft old cheek.

"Why, Jenna, you sweet thing," he said in a shaky voice. "You sure know the way to my heart."

Holding the framed photograph for a long moment, he passed it finally to Duke, whose features also softened when he viewed the protrait of himself and his father that she had taken in the study. She'd had the picture rush printed in sepia tones to bring out its emotional quality.

"Do you have another one of these?" he asked, fixing her with his blue-green gaze.

"I have a black-and-white print at the ranch. You may have it."

Duly passed from hand to hand, the photo was propped upright on the table by Ed T.'s place. When the group finally scattered, Aunt Bliss and Caroline to check last-minute details, Neddy to run an errand, and Duke to talk business with his Uncle Everett, Jenna remained behind with Ed T. She had decided that the occasion of his eightieth birthday would be their last formal interview.

"What's your greatest joy or pride in accomplishment after eight decades of life?" she asked.

"That's easy, honey," he said promptly. "You caught it in that photograph. All my so-called accomplishments in the legislature and in building up our family businesses would add up to nothing in my eyes if there were no Duke to come after me.

"And there almost wasn't. Duke is the greatest joy of my life, a son I can be proud of, my claim to immortality. There was only one person who was closer to me than he is."

He paused and she waited, wondering if, without prodding, he would tell her of Mary Courtenay at last.

"You've never asked about that person," he reminded her.

"I've wanted to," Jenna replied. "I was hoping we could talk about her today."

"You could have anytime. But it's true, sweetheart. Today is right. It won't be like telling a stranger now."

The morning was a cool one, and they sat close together, immersed in their talk and the terrace's shifting light and shadow, Jenna in her cashmere wrap over slacks and a sweater and Ed T. with his lap robe.

Steadily, the old man's voice floated out into the bright air, full of praise and affection for the lovely woman who had come so late and so briefly into his life. His tone was both warm with remembered happiness and sharp with regret. With Jenna he shared the deep, almost painful joy he had known when he'd learned Mary Courtenay was pregnant, the concern with which he had probed all possible solutions to the situation, looking for a way to marry her and protect his child without dishonoring his dead commitment to Elizabeth.

"What I had done seemed both right and wrong to me

at once," he said with a faraway look on his face. "And for the wrong I was punished. While I was still looking for answers, Joe Courtenay came behind my back and took her away. I searched like a wild man. But she and our baby had vanished without a trace."

When he had found Duke again, he'd felt the restoration of his son was a reward for the good in his relationship with Mary. But he'd had to live with the bitter knowledge that only her death had given his son back to him.

"He was such a proud boy when I brought him here, though he'd lived up to that time in poverty," said the old man, remembering. "He had always been called Tom before, after my middle name. But Wayne came up with the nickname Duke because of that strong pride he had. And it stuck."

Jenna smiled softly. "It's not hard to see why."

Ed T. said nothing for a moment, his bright brown eyes searching her face. "You're fond of my boy," he said. "And I sometimes feel you could be a daughter to me. Would you take it as an affront if I spoke frankly?"

"No." Jenna gave the one word response hesitantly, uncertain what would follow.

He laid one big bony hand lightly over hers where it rested beside her coffee cup. "I don't know if you're sleeping with Duke," he said bluntly. "But if you aren't, you soon will be, unless I miss my guess. After that, it's a foregone conclusion. You're a classy, warmhearted woman, like Duke's mother, and he'd be a fool to let you go."

She felt herself flush from the roots of her hair to her collar. But she did not take her gaze away from his.

"Duke's no fool," the old man added. "As for me, I couldn't ask for a better daughter, and I've been waiting a long time to hold a new grandchild on my knee."

Shakily, Jenna leaned forward to kiss his cheek. "Next to my own dad, I can't think of anyone more special than you," she said.

They sat and looked at each other for a long moment, Jenna blinking away tears. She did not trust herself to speak at all on the subject of mothering Duke's child.

"I . . . don't believe Duke is thinking about us in permanent terms," she said finally, "though I don't know him the way you do. If I tell you something, will you keep it secret—absolutely to yourself?"

"Word of honor."

"You might as well know—I'm crazy in love with him."

The old man nodded, satisfied.

"I thought as much," he said. "It showed in the photograph you took. And I'll be mighty surprised if he doesn't feel the same, and tell you so, when you get that story out from between you—it's like a burr in the bedclothes."

The party was a huge success. Guests—relatives, politicians, former law partners, business associates—had flocked to it from around the state and as far away as Washington, D.C., and California. They created a din of conversation and laughter as they filled the old Sanford mansion and crowded forward into the garden room, where the cake was set up, to pay their respects to Ed T.

Jenna recognized the governor of Florida from television news broadcasts—a tanned, middle-aged man with high cheekbones that spoke of Indian blood. She got a good shot of him deep in conversation with the Tyrell patriarch.

She was introduced by Caroline to Ed T.'s niece, Margot Tyrell Jacobson, of Westwood, California, the daughter of the late Burton Tyrell, and Margot's brother, Burton, Jr., a St. Petersburg bank president. Everett's sons Hartley and Philip were also present, as well as the entire Sanford family, including Mary Lou Davies— without her errant congressman.

Naturally, the Howards had come, and Jenna had to admit Vicki, with her cloud of dark auburn hair, looked stunning in a pale lustrous pink silk sheath. She herself had chosen a soft ivory cashmere sweater and skirt, worn with a tiny gold locket that had been her mother's.

She exchanged only a few words with Duke all afternoon. He stayed by his father's side, deftly managing the allotment of time and attention to be given each guest and keeping an eye on things when reporters and cameramen moved in to catch Ed T. cutting his three-tiered, eighty-candle birthday cake.

Not to be outdone, Jenna was in the forefront, snapping twenty or so frames in quick succession. Duke brushed briefly against her as the cake was being served.

"Meet me in the boathouse at four thirty," he whispered in such a low tone she wondered if she'd imagined it.

At about four, Duke reminded his father of doctor's orders and edged him away from the throng. He led him off to a downstairs bedroom at the opposite end of the house that the old man used whenever he was staying in town.

Everett Tyrell went to sit by him and chat awhile before Ed T. slept, since he would be returning to Texas in the morning. Duke didn't reappear at the party right away, and Jenna noted that both Vicki and Mary Lou glanced several times over their shoulders, obviously seeking his tall form in the crowd.

Am I going to be so grateful he prefers my company for the time being that I'll follow orders and arrive promptly to see what he requires of me? she asked herself with a sudden surge of independence.

But then she remembered her promise—not to shy away. Glancing at her watch, she saw that it was four fifteen already. With no compunction, she stole away to put her camera in a drawer and then went out across the lawns.

As she entered the boathouse, the faint talk and laughter of the party drifted toward her from the house. He was waiting for her.

"Duke," she breathed as their arms went around each other.

"I haven't kissed you all day," he reminded her in that deep, softly accented voice of his. "Have you been missing me?"

"Very much. Would you . . . mind doing it now?"

He gave her a quirky little smile of surprise. "You don't have to ask twice, sweetheart."

His mouth was at once passionate and tender, his tongue's sweet probing a taste of the deeper invasion she craved. When the story is finished and not before, if I know him, she thought as she pressed close against him, her arms aching to enfold even more closely his hard, muscular warmth. It's so difficult to wait. I don't know if I'll be able to stand it.

Finally he drew back to look at her, his eyes gleaming at her in the shadowy boathouse.

"Definitely up to standard," he said, then added: "If we go back in together and you stay by me the way I want you to, people are going to get ideas. And that includes just about every member of my family. Will you do it?"

His intentions are ultimately what I'd have called dishonorable before, despite what Ed T. thinks, she decided, standing there intoxicated with him. But I love him so much.

"Of course I will," she said.

The rest of the party passed in a blur, with Jenna only peripherally aware of her rivals' black looks. Almost like a member of the family, she helped direct the cleanup operation afterward and then went with the others to Bern's for a steak dinner.

Ed T. was weary but radiant. Yet both he and Duke expressed some uneasiness at the weather. For Florida, it was a sharply cold night, though the temperature was not expected to go below freezing. On the following night, according to the National Weather Service and Citrus

Mutual, they might not be so lucky. A huge Canadian air mass was pushing southward from the Midwest across the Appalachians and into Georgia.

"The Weather Service says we can expect a low temperature of about twenty-eight degrees," Duke told his father skeptically. "But something tells me it's going to be worse than that—much worse."

Early the next morning a chill northwest wind was blowing as they bade Aunt Bliss good-bye and drove back out to the Bar-T. Immediately, Duke was on the phone, getting in contact with Tyrell Citrus Corporation foremen in groves scattered throughout five counties, from an area just north of Eustis and Tavares in Lake County all the way south to Highlands County and Lake Placid.

As the day lengthened, Weather Service forecasts were repeatedly revised downward, proving his hunch to be correct. Though a warming trend was on the way, it would not save them that night from a killer freeze of sixteen or seventeen degrees.

For the most part, Jenna kept out of the way, her sense of being a part of the family seeming to evaporate. She was finished with her interviews and she had enough photos. There was no excuse to remain.

Yet she knew Duke would object if she talked of leaving, and she realized this was no time to press him. I could start on the writing, she thought. But my deadline is several weeks away. I'd much rather let the story settle.

It was too cold to swim and she finally decided to take one of the horses out on the exercise track that afternoon. When she came in, Neddy and Duke had both gone to bed so that they could be up all night, checking on the groves.

I wonder if he'll ask me to go with him, she thought, deciding on a nap herself. Probably he'll just think I'd be in the way.

But he did ask her, after supper.

"I wouldn't mind the company," he said, "if you can stand a night without sleep. As a journalist, you should find it educational."

By the time they left, the early winter dusk had fallen, and the northwest wind was still blowing in earnest. Jenna had taken her mittens with her and a warm knitted cap Caroline had insisted she would need, as well as an extra sweater to layer under her raincoat. Duke was wearing leather gloves and the fleece-lined jacket she remembered from the night they'd met. He carried a battery-powered weather radio.

"Now you get to see the real Florida, sweetheart," he said. "I hope you like it."

There was time to talk as they sped northward on the interstate to Route 44 and then turned east toward Tavares. Tyrell Corporation groves were situated all throughout Lake and Orange counties on the favored southeast side of Lake Yale, and near Lake Jem and Zellwood and Tangerine. He would make the rounds and see what could be done, Duke explained. But in large measure they were at the mercy of the elements.

"What about smudge pots?" Jenna asked. "I thought those were used to keep the groves warm."

"Not anymore," he replied. "Smudge pots are illegal. We have a few grove heaters that burn kerosene and fuel oil. But they cost the earth to use. We keep them all up here in the north end. If they're predicting seventeen degrees down around Frostproof and Lake Placid, that means Lake and Orange could go as low as ten or twelve."

Jenna shook her head in amazement. "Could it snow?" she asked.

"Seems like it could, doesn't it? But when we get a cold snap, it's usually clear, or only slightly cloudy like tonight, when the wind is blowing. There wouldn't be any freeze if we had a cloud cover to protect us."

In cowboy boots also borrowed from Caroline, Jenna tramped after Duke into the groves, stood beside him in the wide marl furrows between the trees while he talked with his foremen by the light of a kerosene lamp.

"Don't fire up the heaters until it reaches twenty-six degrees," he said to one of them, then added with a grin, "I guess I don't have to tell you that."

At about half past midnight they sped south on Route 27 toward Frostproof. After listening to yet another Weather Service report, Duke switched some country-and-western music on the radio.

"C'mon over here," he said. "It's going to be a long ride."

She cuddled against him. While they drove, the temperature dropped rapidly, so that, by the time they neared the Tyrell property south of Reedy Lake, the average temperature was about twenty-two degrees.

"It'll be down to seventeen or eighteen already in pockets between the ridges," said Duke with a frown. "And with this wind, our wind machines will be useless. About all we'll be able to do is commiserate with each other."

9

`∽∽∽∽∽∽∽∽∽∽∽∽`

"Can't you turn on your irrigation to ward off a freeze?" asked Jenna as they turned in at a gate that bore the Tyrell company sign and went bumping in the Mercedes down a soft, rutted track.

"That isn't done much now, because it can coat the trees too heavily with ice—especially if the cold snap lasts a couple of days—and you lose more in damage to the trees than you gain in saving the crop. The trees are our long-range investment."

By three A.M., they were on their way south again, to an area along the shores of Lake June-in-Winter, south and west of the town of Lake Placid. She could feel Duke's helplessness and frustration mount as they toured the icy groves with no remedy at hand. They huddled round a heater in an equipment shed and listened to more Weather Service reports.

The thermometer read twenty-one degrees.

Finally a watery, pale rose dawn broke in the east, and temperatures began slowly to climb upward. In another hour the freeze would be a thing of the past.

"Well," Duke told his employees finally, "you know what to do. I've got to take this little gal home."

They got in the car. Jenna leaned back, bone weary, against the seat. "Was the damage extensive?" she asked.

He nodded. "I'm afraid so. We'll know more after a while. Usually, there's damage if the temperature stays below twenty-six degrees for about four hours or so. Last night it was below twenty-six for much longer than that."

Jenna closed her eyes as the Mercedes bumped back along the marl track and turned north onto the highway.

"If it's all the same to you," said Duke, "I'll drive as far as Tampa. Then you can have your choice: drive the rest of the way to San Antonio or stop and get some sleep at my apartment."

She didn't look at him. "Your place is fine with me."

Five minutes later she was asleep and dreaming. They were parked in front of his apartment building when he woke her with a gentle shake of her shoulder. She found that in her sleep she had burrowed against him. Even when I'm dead to the world, I feel the pull of him, she thought.

Opening her eyes fully, she realized how tired, almost haggard, he looked. His face was shadowy with beard. Probably that wasn't much of a nap he had yesterday, she thought. And all that driving, while I was asleep.

Though it was still a brisk morning, the Florida sun was shining warmly on frost-wilted schefflera and hibiscus as they walked up to the apartment building's double glass doors.

"Home—sort of," said Duke as they got into the elevator. "I wish we were at Holly Hill this morning. But that bed is going to feel mighty damn fine."

Together, almost like man and wife, they entered the apartment. There was enough sunlight leaking in through the open-weave drapes in the living room for her to really see the place this time—deep blue carpet, paneled walls, a rust-colored sofa in some rough, velvety material, his complex and expensive-looking stereo, a bar.

A love nest. But then, in her wildest dreams she'd never imagined she'd been the first to sleep with him in his wide, comfortable bed. Just the first to do so without making love to him, she added to herself in consternation.

With a quick unreadable glance at her, Duke left her to inspect her surroundings. She heard the shower run briefly, shut off, and then she counted several minutes of silence.

I haven't written one word of the story yet, she thought. Will he relent? Or does he intend for me to stretch out on his couch, leaving the entire bed to him?

"Jenna." The single word was muffled, as if by a pillow.

"Yes?" she called.

"Aren't you coming in?"

A tingle of anticipation reaching to the soles of her feet, she walked into the bedroom. Immediately inside the door, she caught her breath.

He had pulled back the covers and, still naked from the shower, had stretched out on his stomach against the sheet. Though his face was turned into the pillow, she could see that once again he was smooth shaven.

Shy and yet unashamedly ravenous, her gaze traveled the magnificent length of him, sliding over the powerful back and shoulder muscles, his narrow waist and hips. It devoured his trim, neatly shaped buttocks, lighter than his body tan but brown enough that she guessed he had lain out in the sun more than once recently without his swimming trunks.

Holly Hill, she thought. Unsteadily she noted the backs of his hard, sculpted thighs and calves, imagined how those muscles might come into play. . . .

Would he turn over, she wondered, allow her to view his full male glory?

"Jenna?" he asked again, exhaustion edging his voice.

"I'm here."

"God, but I'm tired." He did not open his eyes. "There's a bottle of suntan oil in the medicine cabinet. Would you get it, please?"

Suntan oil? she asked him silently. Tearing her eyes from him, she complied, returning with the bottle in her hand.

"Here it is," she said.

"Good. Now, spread some on my back."

Her little gasp of surprise must have been audible. He half raised his head to look at her, his eyes narrow aquamarine slits.

"I don't have anything better in the place for a massage," he said. "And I ache from head to toe."

For a moment, she was about to sputter in protest at the high-handed way he had commandeered her services. But then she remembered how politely and reasonably he'd asked for the oil and what a night of worry and strain he'd had. Her sympathy went out to him.

Sitting beside him on the bed, she unscrewed the cap of the brown plastic bottle.

"Warm it a little first in the hollow of your hand," he instructed, his eyes closed once more.

She did as he requested.

"All right," he said, "now spread it on my back—in a light, even coat. Use just enough so your hands will move without friction over my skin."

The mental picture his words evoked sent a sharp wave of desire coursing through her. Too easily, she could imagine her palms and fingertips gliding over his back and firmly modeled buttocks, those powerful legs with their dark furring of male body hair.

If he expected her to wait, he was making it awfully rough on her.

"What's the matter?" he asked, his voice holding a faint note of amusement. "Don't you like touching me?"

"I'm not going to answer that," she snapped, certain he had read her thoughts. Then she added, more softly, "You know the answer anyway."

With trembling fingers, she spread the warmed tanning preparation, redolent of coconut oil, over the bare skin of his shoulders and back. She stroked it from the nape of his neck, just under the blunt-cut ends of his thick dark hair, to his lean waist.

Hesitating slightly, she continued her downward movement, molding her hands to the curve of his lean hips, his legs. Oil caught and glistened in the hair that so softly covered his hard, muscled limbs.

"You'll need another shower," she said, her voice coming out throaty and breathless, like a stranger's.

"Not until after we sleep."

"I have to put some more of this on your shoulders," she replied as offhandedly as she could.

Resuming her unspoken communication with him, she couldn't seem to stop the errant way her hands wanted to caress him—sinews and shoulder blades, the little hollows along his spine. To touch him this way made her burn with longing.

He gave a small sigh of pleasure. "That feels wonderful, sweetheart," he said. "You really know now to handle a man. Now, get on me and really put some muscle into it. Take off your boots and those scratchy jeans first. And your cashmere sweater, unless you want the sleeves coated with oil."

Am I to undress at his command? she thought with indignation, forgetting that she had been silently entertaining equally scandalous wishes only moments before. But, almost as if she had no will of her own, she found herself tugging off her boots and stockings, unzipping her relatively new blue jeans and sliding them from her hips to step free. Pausing briefly, she pulled the sweater over her head.

"Sit on the backs of my thighs," Duke directed. "Something tells me you've never given a massage before."

Softly, her shyness increasing again, she admitted he was right. The notion of sitting astride him in this state had aroused a tumult of emotions that threatened to overpower her. Yet she could hardly refuse—did not want to refuse.

In thin silk camisole top and panties, with a quickening response she could not suppress, she lowered herself onto Duke's hard thighs, pressing her own thighs against his lean hips.

"Innocent," he jibed tenderly with a note in his voice that might have been satisfaction. "I'll tell you what to do."

Like one possessed, she followed the instructions he gave her in his deep, soft voice, losing some of her trepidation as she threw the weight of her torso into the strokes he requested instead of using mere muscle power. Kneading with the heels of her hands and the balls of her thumbs, she moved upward from points just to the left and right of the base of his spine to his shoulders. Then she made tiny circles between vertebrae up the length of his spine to rake little downward furrows on either side of it with the fore and middle fingers of each hand.

Duke was giving little groans of contentment.

"Now my shoulder blades," he said, "and then my neck and shoulders. Don't be afraid to press."

He raised each shoulder blade in turn for her to trace the hollow around it. She could feel the tension knotted in his neck and shoulders. Without any direction from him now, she let her affection for him mold her hands and fingers to the contours of his body. They seemed to sense his tension and gently disperse it.

"Heavenly," he sighed, his voice now very low. "Would you mind doing my lower back again?"

With a deepening pleasure in the process, she granted his wish, this time using her forearms to make contact as well as her hands and fingers. Then, thrusting all notions of propriety aside, she allowed herself to stroke his hips, knead his firm buttocks. Moving off him and to one side, she applied a light hacking stroke to the length of his legs and then returned to an all-over rubbing of his back and shoulders.

I wish I dared to lay my cheek down against him, she thought. Or to kiss him where my hands have traveled, the way I want. How can I be expected to touch him this way and remain unmoved? If he doesn't turn over soon and take me into his arms, press me into the mattress with the weight of him, I won't be able to stand it.

"Duke?" she whispered at last, gently slackening the rhythm of her hands on his warm, oil-scented skin.

There was no answer. His breath came softly and evenly, and she could not discern even a flutter of his dark eyelashes as they lay against his cheeks. He had fallen fast asleep!

I can't bear it, she thought in anguished disappointment, resting her palms against him. I know he's tired. But I want him so much. . . .

She didn't know what to do. Probably I should go lie down on the sofa after all, she reasoned, casting her eye about for a spare blanket. But she knew how prim and foolish that would seem, when the bed was big enough for them both and they had shared it once before. The only problem with remaining beside him—and it was a major one—involved the pain of her unfulfilled desire.

With a deep sigh, she disengaged herself from him as gently as she could. Suddenly it seemed the height of silliness that she was wearing anything at all. Shedding the camisole top and panties, she lay down beside him and pulled up the top sheet and blanket.

At least we'll sleep together, she thought. But it was a long time before she drifted into slumber.

When she woke, she was in his arms, her head pillowed in the hollow of his shoulder, one hand resting on that silky mat of chest hair under the blanket. Their legs were all tangled up together. With a little start, she realized his eyes were open and he was looking at her.

"Hello, sweetheart," he said softly. "In case you're wondering, it's three o'clock in the afternoon."

"We've slept . . ."

"Five hours. Thanks to that wonderful massage, it will be enough. You know, I really could get in the habit of sleeping with you."

Oh, thought Jenna. Tell me about it. She realized he was waiting for her to respond.

"At first I . . . didn't know what to do when you fell asleep," she admitted finally. "Whether to stay beside you or not. But I have to confess—at the moment, it feels exactly right."

"Good." His arms tightened about her. "I like a woman who says what she feels. And I especially like the way you feel to me in nothing but your lovely satin skin."

Smoothing the length of her back, he lifted her chin with one finger to nuzzle her mouth, teasing it open with his tongue. Though his kiss was languid, almost lazy, it telegraphed a pulse-quickening message: she was about to get her wish.

"Duke," she whispered, as his mouth strayed to nip at one ear's tender lobe. "It nearly killed me when you fell asleep that way."

"Darling. Let me make it up to you."

His mouth traced a path to her breasts to tug and pull at them tenderly, as his hands went on touching her under the blanket.

"If I can't have you this time, Duke, I'll die."

She didn't realize she had spoken aloud.

"You'll have me, sweetheart—never fear," he promised thickly, returning his plundering mouth to hers. "Wild horses couldn't drag me away from you now."

He kissed her again, a kiss as deep as time itself, rapacious and yet so loving she wept.

"But I want us to slow down, so our first time together will be wonderful, darling," he added, his smoky turquoise eyes now narrow slits. "I want you to feel every quiver of excitement and pleasure I'm capable of arousing in you, every sweet stab of longing."

He pulled back the blanket. With a studied finesse that spoke of his experience, he set about arousing her even more, until she cried out with the sensations he was evoking in her.

Desire, blazing and yet as mindless and rhythmic as the

sea, washed over her in ever more towering waves. On her stomach and thighs, his kisses fed the conflagration within.

Out of control, she let passion take charge of her movements, daring to touch him as he was touching her, caressing his hard male body and drawing him toward her emptiness. He groaned in surprise and pleasure.

"All right, darling," he conceded, his voice husky beyond recognition as he parted her thighs and came fully into her embrace. "You know I can't hold out against you."

Arching to meet him, she rubbed the sensitized soles of her feet against his calves as she felt him seeking against her. In the next second he had found her, to plunge into her with a deep, full thrust that seemed to reach into her very soul.

"Duke," she cried softly, her hands digging into his shoulders. "Oh, Duke . . ."

For a moment, he held her tightly, as if exercising over himself an iron control he had momentarily lost.

"I've got all of you now, Jenna," he whispered, his breath hot in her ear.

"Oh, yes. Darling, I want you to . . ."

Words became superfluous a moment later when his renewed thrusting prompted her to an inborn, rhythmic movement Paul had never evoked. She was like a well, as deep as the earth, and yet he filled her. Still she needed more from him, more, as she strove against him to give him everything she could. Their aching half-selves made whole, they mounted slowly, inexorably to the peak of their communion.

Yet it surprised her when it came. Suddenly she was flooded with a great warmth of almost unbearable pleasure. Almost as quickly, she broke free, into total abandonment, lost in the cascading spasms of delight that wracked her body from head to toe.

Unaware of what she did, she half-rose from the pillow

to press herself against his chest. At the same time, Duke was transformed by his own ecstasy, his powerful body shuddering repeatedly against her.

Finally, they stilled. Collapsing in her arms, he pressed her to the mattress as they floated, without thought or any wish to draw apart, in the warm sea of pleasure that still surrounded them. She had never felt so complete.

At last, Duke rolled off her, gently, almost reluctantly, and drew her against him so that her head was resting on his shoulder.

"Now, darling," he said, his voice deep with his own contentment, "let's go back to sleep."

She woke again at almost five. Duke's place was empty beside her. Rolling onto her side, she saw that he was sitting, comfortably naked, in a blue velour chair and talking on the phone. Her man.

"All right," he said to someone as he curled his free hand around a shot glass of some pale golden liquid, probably Scotch. "I was going to call them next anyway. See you later. And . . . thanks for a good job last night."

Replacing the receiver, he came over to her and kissed her.

"Sleep well?" he asked, his eyes gleaming at the natural way her arms slipped around him.

Jenna nodded, loving him even more than before, if that were possible. "It was wonderful," she said.

"You don't have to tell me, sweetheart." He paused, frowning at her faintly. "But I'm not sure we should have . . . made love before you finish your story. I don't want you to think . . ."

"That you're trying to bribe me?"

He grinned. "Not that. What I tried to do to you that first night."

She shook her head. "It wouldn't work now. Where you're concerned, I have no shame."

"That's as it should be if you're my girl." Something flickered in his eyes. "But I think maybe we'd better take it easy for a while," he added, "until that hellacious story is complete. Why don't you get dressed and I'll take you out for some dinner."

Hiding her disappointment, she nodded, then asked if he had heard from the ranch yet.

"I was just going to call them. It seems they've been trying to get me all afternoon."

Her brow furrowed in puzzlement. "Why didn't they try here? The phone didn't ring . . ."

"That's because I pulled it out of the jack. Go on now. Get ready while I give them a ring."

Seating himself again in the blue chair, he dialed the Bar-T.

"Hi," he said to someone as she picked up her jeans and sweater and headed for the shower. "How are things going?"

When she emerged, dressed and ready to go except for her shoes, he was still on the phone and frowning deeply.

"Have you called the doctor?" he was asking. "Considering Ed T.'s age, I think he should be in on this."

What's wrong? she mouthed at him and then stood by with growing uneasiness as he motioned her to keep still.

"All right," he said finally. "I'm glad you did that. Don't worry. I'll be home right away." With a brief good-bye, he replaced the receiver.

"That was Caroline," he said, anticipating her questions. "Ed T. got Wayne to take him up into the groves in the golf cart and he was out there most of the night. Now he's complaining of dizziness and chest pain and coming down with a bad cold."

"Oh, no." Jenna's frown now matched his own.

"At his age, and with his heart, a cold could be risky," Duke acknowledged, his note of concern deepening. "Like a sensible girl, Caroline called Doc Glidewell, and he's with him now. But I've got to get back out there. Our dinner will have to wait."

"Of course," said Jenna promptly, pulling on her socks. "We have to make sure he's okay."

He gave her shoulders a brief, hard squeeze. "You're my girl, aren't you?" he asked.

"Yes," she said with quiet pride. I wish I could be your girl, she thought, all my life.

Kissing her lightly on the cheek, he began to dress rapidly.

"By the way," he added tonelessly, "Ed T.'s getting sick isn't the only bad news. Paco Nuñez just died."

Tears slid down her cheeks and he put his arms around her and held her for a moment.

"I'm sorry," he said. "I understand how you feel. But we knew it was coming. Ed T.'s going to be okay."

She nodded, drying her eyes. "Your father," she said. "I love him too."

"I know you do," Duke replied.

On the afternoon of Paco's funeral, they took Ed T. into Tampa to the hospital. Despite all they had tried to do, the cold had developed into pneumonia. Duke had ridden with his father in the ambulance, while Jenna followed with Caroline in the Mercedes. Neddy, ashen-faced and shaken, had gone to speak to Aunt Bliss. It seemed like the whole world had come tumbling down around their ears.

At the hospital, Jenna parked the car in the nearest available space. Not bothering to lock it, she ran with Caroline up the concrete entrance ramp of the emergency room in time to see Ed T. being wheeled away toward the elevator.

There was a bevy of nurses about him and a green plastic oxygen mask covering his face. The bomblike oxygen bottle hung from a metal rack above the cart. Duke's jaw was set and she knew at once that here was a situation in which he was at a loss, one he did not instinctively know how to master.

"They're taking him up to the cardiac unit because of

135

his heart condition," he informed them quickly, as he turned to follow. "Third floor, east. They'll have him on a respirator in a minute and that should help." Then he was gone.

"Is . . . the doctor up there?" asked Caroline in a pitifully small voice. Her face had that shocked, almost bruised look people get when the impossible happens and someone loved, who is expected to live forever, is suddenly in mortal danger.

Jenna put an arm around her shoulders, felt them shaking. "If Doctor Glidewell isn't here yet, he will be any minute," she said. "And Duke said something before leaving the ranch about calling in a specialist. Your grandfather will be better off here, Caroline."

The younger girl leaned against her. "It nearly killed me to see him facing backward like that in the ambulance all the way to Tampa," she confessed suddenly, the tears that hadn't come during that long, harrowing trip now rolling down her cheeks. "It was—oh, I don't know—ignominious somehow. He should ride facing forward, like in that picture of him on the mantel in his study, as a young man on his favorite horse—or even in the golf cart."

Caroline's voice broke and she began to sob in earnest. Jenna put both arms around her, holding her until she quieted. She knew people in the emergency waiting room were staring at them, wondering if someone had died. Just please don't let it be true, Jenna prayed, for Duke's and Caroline's sake.

"Excuse me, miss." A young intern with fiery red hair was standing beside them. "I believe your party has gone upstairs. Wouldn't it be better to go up there and wait?"

At his suggestion, they collected themselves and headed for the elevators.

"He . . . said that like this . . . was a restaurant," said Caroline with a watery little attempt at a smile.

"Yes," said Jenna, trying to smile back as best she

could while she pressed the third-floor button. "Don't let's borrow trouble. Duke says Ed T. is going to be okay."

"I hope so." Caroline took a tissue from her purse and blew her nose. "But you know, don't you," she added, "that Duke isn't always right?"

Only scant information was available from the cardiac unit nurse. "The doctor and Mr. Tyrell are with him," she said. "I'm sorry, but the two of you will have to wait in the lounge at the end of the corridor. We'll let you know as soon as we hear anything."

There was nothing else to do or say. Time passed slowly, and it seemed hours before Duke came out to them. Caroline had curled up into a miserable little heap in the corner of the lounge's Danish modern sofa to leaf dejectedly through a pile of dog-eared magazines. Finally, she shut her eyes.

In a chair beside her, Jenna was staring at a cheap print of Van Gogh's *Starry Night* that hung on the opposite wall, monotonously tracing the pinwheel stars with her eyes. It's enough to drive you mad, she thought, a terrible choice for a hospital. They should have a picture with green pastures. And still waters, her tired mind prodded. *Thou lead'st me beside the still waters. . . .* Oh, no, God, she pleaded silently. Don't let Ed T. die.

"Jenna."

She looked up to see Duke standing beside her. Caroline also opened her eyes.

"How is he?" they asked, almost in unison.

Duke's face still wore its grim look, and his effort to sustain a mask of confidence tore at Jenna's heart.

"Holding his own," he said, his deep voice carefully even. "Being a Tyrell, he's a fighter. But one lung has collapsed and the other is congested. There's an irregular heartbeat . . ."

Caroline was on her feet and into his arms. "Duke," she cried softly against his leather jacket. "You can't let anything happen to him."

"I'm doing my level best to prevent it, honey." Patting her gently, he reached out to squeeze Jenna's hand.

"I have to go back inside," he said finally. "If you two want to go on down to Ballast Point . . ."

Jenna looked at Caroline. "We'll stay here," she said.

"Good. I like having you nearby." Kissing each of them lightly on the cheek, he went back down the hall with his long, quick strides and disappeared into Ed T.'s room.

About twenty minutes later, Neddy joined them, strung out, to sit opposite Jenna under the Van Gogh print and chain-smoke. Suppertime came and went, marked only by the arrival of food carts on the floor. They had no appetite.

The passage of time was marked by the waiting-room clock, the bells, the doctors' pages on the hospital intercom, and Duke's hourly reports. The reports were always the same: no change.

Finally the three of them went down for coffee, letting the floor nurse know where they could be reached. Served in a Styrofoam cup, the coffee was bitter and murky and only upset Jenna's stomach. Tossing the container into a trash barrel as they departed to go back upstairs, she realized she had nervously chewed the rim into a pattern.

About ten o'clock, Duke came out to report that Ed T. was resting a little more comfortably, although he was still in considerable danger. His fever had edged down some, though his breathing, even with the respirator, was raspy and difficult.

"I think it's safe for you all to go home and get some rest," he said.

"You're staying here?" Neddy put the question.

Duke nodded. "When you come back in the morning, Jenna," he added, "please bring my razor. I keep a spare one at Aunt Bliss's."

Aunt Bliss, with her stiff Tyrell backbone, welcomed

them like lost lambs despite her own overwhelming concern for her brother's welfare.

But Jenna didn't get much rest. Caroline had asked to share a room with her, and the younger girl's tossing kept her awake. So did her desperate prayers for Ed T. and her thoughts of Duke, sitting beside his father in the hospital. Aching with concern for him, she remembered the way it had been at his apartment, how their ecstatic coming together had made them almost one person.

They had not made love since, had scarcely even had a private moment together. I just want to hold him now, she thought. Nothing more. I just want to be there when he needs me. When she did fall asleep, it was to struggle with uneasy dreams.

By morning, Ed T.'s condition had not improved. Duke's eyes had a haunted look as he accepted the razor and went to shave in his father's washroom.

Again Jenna and Caroline sat in the waiting room together, the latter crocheting a halter top to have something to do with her hands. Neddy, who'd had far too much to drink the night before, according to Thalia Jones, didn't join them until noon. His eyes were bloodshot, and for once he had little to say.

The prognosis wasn't good. Despite his strong will, Ed T. was eighty years old and his body had begun to give way. At first, Duke tried not to let on what was happening, hoping against hope that his father would rally. But then, when Neddy had gone for another pack of cigarettes and Caroline had fallen asleep, he asked Jenna to walk with him down the corridor.

She slipped her arm about his waist, not knowing what to say.

"I guess I can tell you, sweetheart," he said in a voice like no other she'd heard from him. "We're losing him."

"Duke," she said, and then: "Darling, are you sure?"

He nodded. "I hope I'm wrong. But I'm going to call Everett."

She put both arms around him, her eyes brimming with tears that she willed not to spill over. "What can I do?"

For a moment, he held her tightly, his face buried in her hair. "Just stick around," he said, still in that terrible voice. "I'm going to need you."

Jenna stood by him while he telephoned, heard him say the awful words that did not, could not, seem real. When he hung up, he dialed Aunt Bliss and gave her the news.

"Let the rest of the family know how things stand," he told her. "I'm going back in to be with him."

At four o'clock it was all over. A sudden, massive coronary attack had finished what the pneumonia had begun. Not all the modern medical technology in the hospital or his son's strong will could save Ed T.

"Take Caroline home," Duke instructed Neddy, his aquamarine eyes gone opaque and the realization of loss beginning to replace disbelief in his face. "Jenna will stay here with me."

Tears were streaming down Neddy's face and he didn't bother to wipe them away. "Why should you be the one?" he said. "Always you. I barely got into the room while he was still alive."

Duke betrayed no emotion. "I'm his next of kin," he said. "I have to sign the papers."

With a little sob, Neddy turned away.

All Jenna could offer was her wordless presence as Duke completed the necessary forms and other business. She waited in the corridor while he went into Ed T.'s room to say good-bye.

When he came out, his eyes were suspiciously wet. But she knew better than to put her arms around him then. She merely handed him the car keys and let him take her hand in a bone-crushing grip.

It was nearly dusk when they reached Ballast Point. Behind its hedges, the old house was brightly lit. Aunt Bliss will be preparing for another onslaught of relatives, she thought, partly because she doesn't know what else to do.

For Jenna, none of it yet seemed real. The old man couldn't be gone. But with her parents and Andy, there hadn't even been this much warning. Just a telephone call, an unexpected visit, the look on her uncle's face.

It can't *be*, thought Jenna, her own grief for Ed T. welling up. It's almost like losing them all over again. She got control of herself with difficulty.

"Whatever you need, darling, just ask," she told Duke softly as he went into the study to pour himself a stiff drink and get on the telephone. "I'll be with Caroline."

Somehow, by cajoling and setting an example, Jenna got Caroline to eat a few mouthfuls of one of Thalia Jones's best chicken salad sandwiches and drink some hot chocolate.

"I won't believe Granddad is gone," Caroline whispered in a quavering voice as she let Jenna pull a blanket over her and hold her like a mother or a sister. "I . . . can't imagine life without him."

"You aren't really without him, you know," Jenna replied, remembering a poem someone had given her in her own darkest hour. "A poet once said that the influence of someone he loved who had died just 'entered the air' and stayed all around him. Your grandfather's influence and love will always surround you, Caroline."

For a moment, her only reply was a fierce hug. "I wish you were my sister," the younger girl said. "But . . . maybe you'll be my aunt instead. My Uncle Duke's in love with you, isn't he?"

Jenna bit her lip, a study in mixed emotion. She was grateful that the lamplight was turned low.

"If he is, he hasn't told me about it," she said as lightly as she could.

"He is—I know him." For the space of a second, Caroline sounded very like her grandfather. Then: "You do love him too, don't you?" she asked anxiously.

Caroline's need for reassurance was very real and Jenna felt compelled to honesty.

"Very much," she said. "His beautiful eyes and dark hair and broad shoulders. That wicked smile. Just everything."

Relaxing a little, Caroline closed her eyes. "That's good," she said. "We'll be all right if we have you."

10

Kissing Caroline lightly on the forehead, she turned out the lamp and went softly out, promising to return. As she went downstairs in search of Duke, she found her mind couldn't assimilate Caroline's assertion that she, Jenna, might somehow heal the gaping wound in the family caused by the old man's death. All she wanted at the moment was to find the man she loved and put her arms around him.

The Mercedes was gone from the drive in front of the house, and her heart sank for a moment until she realized Tomás had probably put it in the garage. Still, she couldn't find Duke anywhere.

Aunt Bliss was in the garden room, quietly drinking tea among her beloved plants.

"Have you seen Duke?" Jenna asked, and then felt a fool. The old woman would be grieving too.

"I'm sorry," she said. "I guess I'm not being very tactful this evening. Are you all right, Aunt Bliss? Is there anything I can do?"

Bliss Sanford's mouth softened slightly.

"You mustn't worry about me, my dear," she said. "I'm an old woman. And, according to my belief, I'll be seeing Ed T. long before the rest of you."

She paused. "If you want to do something," she added, "go after that man of yours. I expect you'll find him in the boathouse."

Giving Aunt Bliss an eloquent look, Jenna went out through the garden room doors. The grass was wet with dew as she crossed the lawn under the dark shapes of the trees.

"Duke," she called softly, pushing the creaking boathouse door open a little.

There was no reply. All she could make out in the darkness inside was the dim outline of the Tyrell yacht hanging motionless from its huge davits. Yet someone had partly opened the overhead door to the bay and she could see the sheen of the water.

"Darling," she tried again. "Please let me be with you."

She caught a slight movement inside the large rubber raft that was stashed to one side of the boathouse. She remembered noting it briefly on the day of Ed T.'s party.

"Better not stay, Jenna," Duke said, his deep voice rough with sorrow. "Unless you want to see a grown man cry."

"Oh, sweetheart, I wouldn't mind."

She was beside him in an instant, lying down with him in the raft to take him in her arms. He held her tightly, desperately, so fiercely she almost thought her ribs would break.

"Jenna, oh, my God," he said brokenly, his face buried against her breast. "I can't *bear* it. To lose him. I just can't believe it's true."

She couldn't offer words. Instead, she cradled his head, her fingers meshed in his thick, dark hair, feeling the great sobs that wracked his body, his tears hot and wet against her shirt, soaking through to her skin.

Her own tears were falling heedlessly. Duke, darling, I love you so, she told him silently. I'd give anything if I could bring him back for you.

At last, he quieted, though he still held tightly to her, as if to a life preserver. She wondered if they would spend the night thus, to fall asleep in each other's arms. She was willing—even if it did cause a scandal with the rest of the family.

"Jenna." He lifted his head and met her eyes finally in the dark.

"Yes?" she whispered.

"I'm glad, after all, that we made love that day. I'd be so empty now, so alone, if it weren't for you."

She said nothing, thinking of what they had shared and of all the women who wanted him, who would fight each other for the chance to help him mend his sorrow. But he's right about one thing, she admitted to herself. None of them could love him the way I do.

"Say you won't leave me. Say you won't go away now because there'll be no more interviews."

To her surprise, his voice held the same note of uncertainty she'd caught after that first unsettling phone call about Ed T.'s illness.

"I . . . won't, if you need me."

"Rest assured, sweetheart, I do." He paused. "You weren't thinking about going, were you?"

"No," she said.

But I can't just forget my assignment and the fact that I'm not really a member of this family, she added silently. I can't stay on here indefinitely as "Duke's girl." Is that what he expects?

But, even if he wanted nothing more from her, she knew she'd never turn away.

"As long as you want or need me," she responded, "I'll be here."

A muscle jerked beside his mouth. "Is that a promise?"

She nodded.

"Say it," he requested.

"I promise, Duke."

His arms tightened around her. "You might be staying a long time, then. Ed T. . . ."

He winced, leaving his intended remark unmade. "God," he groaned instead. "My father was like a part of me. It's like a big piece of me has been torn away. I can't get used to it."

145

"I know," she said. "It was easy to see . . . what a special feeling there was between you. The morning of his birthday, I asked him a few last questions—about his greatest source of pride and accomplishment in his long life. He pointed to that picture I'd taken, said it was all there, between the two of you."

Unashamedly his tears spilled again, more softly now. "Thank you," he said, not bothering to hide the catch in his voice. "That's like giving me back something of him to keep."

"Darling, you're welcome. But you've got a lot more than that, right inside yourself. You're exactly like him, in so many ways. His immortality, he said."

He was silent a long moment. "In that case, I have a debt to pay," he said, considering. "I need a sweet Mary Courtenay of my own to bear *me* a son . . ."

She did not trust herself to speak. Her body suddenly ached with her devastatingly real longing to be that person.

"It may not be the time to tell you so," he added. "But I like the way you kept calling me darling tonight. It tugged me back from the edge of my grief more than once."

Again she didn't know what to say.

He placed a soft little kiss on her mouth. "Now I think you should be going back to the house," he said.

"And you?"

"I'll walk with you as far as the terrace. But, since I can't just take you up to my bed and hold you the way I've been doing for the past hour, I'm going to stay outside a while longer."

She shot him a glance.

In response, the corners of his mouth lifted faintly. "Don't worry, Jenna," he said. "Thanks to you, I'll be okay."

On the day of Ed T.'s funeral it rained, a rare occurrence that dry winter. They were seated in St.

Andrew's Episcopal Church, Jenna with the family at Duke's insistence, when they heard the first roll of thunder.

By the time the long line of black limousines and cars was winding up the interstate to Brooksville and Holly Hill, where Ed T. would be buried beside Mary Courtenay in the estate's tiny Civil War cemetery, the heavens had opened. It was raining in solid gray sheets, the way it can only in Florida, and the water was coming down so hard they could barely make out the flashing taillights of the hearse that bore Ed T.'s body. Lightning, in great huge forks, split the gloom periodically, to be followed by Olympian peals of thunder, rumbling away into echoes.

Neddy and Everett sat on either side of Aunt Bliss in the limousine, Duke—looking somber and taller than ever in a dark suit and tie—between Jenna and Caroline. Duke's arm was around his niece's shoulder. He held tightly to Jenna's hand, but this morning his strong, beautiful features were composed.

Rain was falling softly, the worst of the storm behind them, as the cortege turned up the narrow track and passed through Holly Hill's whimsical iron gates. To Jenna, the house had lost its expectant air. But, conversely, it seemed all the more timeless.

In the shuffle of parking the cars and crossing the lawns in a crowd of people, she managed to slip away from the Tyrells. That morning, feeling like a traitor but knowing that professionally she must do it, she had put her Nikon and its distance lens in the large leather purse she carried.

Maybe none of the pictures she would get that day would ever be published. But, if by chance she captured the essence of what she was feeling and what the story would say, she would allow Paul to use the photographs —even if Duke hated her for it.

She could think of no better way to show the strong love Ed T.'s family and friends felt for him, no more fitting tribute. I love your son, Ed T., she said to the old man in her mind as she switched off the motor drive and adjusted the F-stop for natural light. But I must be my own woman and do what's right. You would understand.

Ed T. had been a figure of statewide significance, and several of the same television stations and newspapers that had covered his birthday party had assigned staffers to the funeral. Tying a dark printed challis scarf over her hair and huddling in her raincoat, she hoped she would be mistaken for one of the other reporters if any of the Tyrells happened to see her. Duke would be missing her, she knew, but he'd also be preoccupied.

I am taking advantage of him, she thought with a stab of guilt. I should have told him what I intended.

But it was too late now. Camouflaging herself in the crowd, she zoomed in on family and notables, the flower-decked coffin, Duke's face, which had taken on the bruised, daunted look Caroline's had worn at the hospital.

Then, when the last rites were finished and the coffin was being lowered into the earth, she put away camera and scarf, opened her black umbrella, and went to stand behind him. He felt her presence almost immediately, half-turned, and drew her forward to stand beside him. How many people saw what I was doing, she thought, and wonder how he can allow it? She caught a swift glance from Neddy and realized, *He knows.*

"Where have you been?" Duke whispered.

"Here," she said. "In the crowd."

There was no time to say anything more. Duke stepped forward to throw the first shovelful of earth on the casket. When it came her turn, Jenna did the same. Good-bye, Ed T., she whispered silently to herself. I hope I am doing what you would have wished.

Very quickly, it was over, and the mourners were dispersing back to their cars. Duke had ordered that the Holly Hill house not be opened that day, and those relatives and close friends who would join the family later would do so back at Bliss Sanford's house.

Everett helped Aunt Bliss back to the family's limousine, but Duke, Neddy, and Caroline, with Jenna beside them, remained standing at the graveside for some minutes, even though the rain had quickened again.

"I don't want to turn my back and walk away," said Duke finally, his light, blue-green eyes clear though they spoke eloquently of his pain. "But it's just an illusion that we can keep him now." Putting an arm about each of them, he walked Jenna and Caroline back to the car, leaving Neddy to follow.

For the next forty-eight hours they were seldom alone. Everett and several of Duke's cousins who had come for the funeral remained at the house, and there was barely a chance to speak privately.

Duke had immediately assumed control of his father's stock in the family corporation, as Ed T.'s will provided, and he was on the phone a great deal, reassuring business contacts and catching up with a backlog of problems.

But, by the third morning after the funeral, all of the cousins had gone. And, when Jenna came down early to breakfast, she found that, instead of being closeted in the study with guests or on the telephone, Duke was sitting at the table, reading his morning paper over coffee.

"Sweetheart, I have a proposition for you," he said quietly before she could speak. "I have to get away where I can think, and I need you beside me. Will you come with me to Holly Hill?"

She nodded, wondering what was on his mind. More than anything, now, she wanted to be alone with him, just to hold him or talk with him if that was all he wanted.

"It won't bother me being so near . . . where Ed T. is buried," he said in answer to her unspoken question. "He's with Mary anyway, and I'm the living owner of the place. But I might want to talk about him some, think my random thoughts out loud to somebody who'll understand. Maybe even cry a few more tears."

"When do we leave?"

"In about twenty minutes. Or will it take you longer to get your things together?"

She paused, about to help herself to biscuits and marmalade.

"Not including breakfast," he added with a hint of his old smile. "You'd put that biscuit back if I wanted you to, wouldn't you, and toddle off to Brooksville hungry?"

"Maybe so," she said with a little smile of her own. "Though I might not always be as docile as you suggest."

But it was a *pro forma* objection. In her heart she knew she couldn't deny him anything at the moment. He'd been through so much. And he looked so appealing and almost boyish that morning in his tan corduroy jeans and checked shirt, wearing the same pair of quality leather boots she'd stomped on with her stiletto heel.

His dark hair appeared just washed and springy to the touch. Those heartbreakingly beautiful aquamarine eyes were glinting at her from beneath dark lashes. Even the shape of his hands around the coffee cup is enough to turn my head, she thought. But then, I know firsthand how much pleasure those hands can give.

"If you keep looking at me like that," said Duke, "I'm not going to wait until you finish your breakfast."

"Looking . . . how?"

"You know. By the way, the weather's warmed up considerably so I called my groundskeeper yesterday and had him heat up the pool. You'd better throw in a suit if you plan to wear one."

He turned serious again in the car, drawing her tightly against him, not so much in a sexual way, but as if he wanted her human nearness and warmth. To her surprise, he spent most of the hour's drive north speaking of Ed T. and the way he had felt about him as a child. Never once using the phrase *off the record*, he acted quite as if she'd agreed to drop her project.

But he must know better than that, she thought.

"Mary described Ed T. to me when I was only about

five years old," he told her, keeping his eyes on the road. "That was after Joe Courtenay had left us for good. We were living in a walk-up apartment over a grocery store in Asheville and she was working as a seamstress. She told me straight out that he was my real father and how that had come about.

"I didn't realize then that people would think it was a scandal. I only remember wondering why we couldn't go to live with him, if he loved us so much."

Jenna didn't comment, but just laid her hand on his knee in the way he liked.

"Three years later," he said, "when she got so sick, she wrote my father a letter. I was not allowed to read it, but she made me promise to mail it if anything happened to her. I carried it with me day and night, slept with it under my pillow.

"Then, when Mary died, I posted it. She had arranged with her landlady to keep me until my father came. A few days later, he arrived—so tall, it seemed then, and older than I'd expected. But warm. And so . . . big and powerful, as if he could control the world. I knew immediately that we belonged together. . . ."

His voice trailed off and he was silent a moment, remembering.

"Ed T. said you were a very proud boy when he brought you home," put in Jenna softly. "He told me how Wayne came up with your nickname."

Duke's mouth relaxed a little, as if in faint amusement at himself. "I had to live up to him, and to being a Tyrell," he said. "But I guess, if the truth be known, pride is just a part of my nature. I remember telling you once that I can be boorish and arrogant."

"I haven't forgotten." Taking her hand from his knee, Jenna slipped her arm around him. "I like you just the way you are," she said.

Sunlight dappled through the trees as Duke turned up the Holly Hill drive. This time he pulled the Mercedes up to the veranda steps.

"This is part of why I wouldn't allow the house to be opened the other day," he said. "I didn't want us to have that kind of memory."

Getting out, he held her door and then took their things out of the trunk to set them on the porch. As he opened the screen and fitted his key into the lock, Jenna had the most curious feeling of coming home. Without benefit of matrimony, she thought. But home, nonetheless. She knew they were finally at the place where, above all others, he had wanted to make love to her.

Inside, a hall with soft board planks, worn, narrow Oriental runners, and a tall old clock ran from front to back porches to catch every breeze. Without suggesting a tour of parlor or library, Duke gave her a questioning look and carried their bags up the broad, creaking Victorian staircase. With a little shiver of anticipation, she followed.

At the top, he hesitated a moment, then opened a door. "I think you should sleep in Mary's room," he told her, again with that faintly quizzical look.

He had not said "we." Uncertainly and with a kind of reverence, Jenna surveyed the high old four-poster bed of rich mahogany, the pier glass on its stand, a tall mahogany armoire, and a wicker rocker, the latter placed by the floor-to-ceiling windows. It was just as she'd imagined it.

On the room's bare floors were scattered several lacy straw carpets. He put her cases by the bed.

"Are you . . . sure you want me to sleep here?" she asked. She didn't voice the question that was really bothering her: Aren't we going to sleep together?

His next words answered neither question. "Do whatever you need about unpacking and then come walking with me. I want your company."

In the bedroom itself there were no closets, and she quickly put away the few things she'd brought in the mahogany wardrobe. In the jeans and old yellow sweater she'd worn for the trip, her hair plaited in a single blond-streaked braid, she joined him downstairs on the veranda.

"Jenna," he said simply, putting an arm about her waist.

Even when she grew old someday, she thought, she would not forget the sounds and sights and scents of that morning and afternoon—the clear soft insistent calls of the birds hidden in the lush foliage, the bitter green earth smell of moss and gingery aroma of some flower he couldn't name, the way leaves in a tall, leggy grove of bamboo flickered in the breeze.

"Even in the hottest part of the summer, there's always a breeze here," Duke told her as they brushed beneath papery, rustling palm fronds.

Always through the trees there were glimpses of the hazy blue distance. With the breeze came little rushes of quiet in which they seemed to speak in lowered voices or not to talk at all. From a moss-draped branch would come a rhythmical *tweet-tweet-tweet-tweet-tweet*, followed by a sharp *bob-white*. Then an insect chorus, shrilly beautiful, would break the spell.

Ed T. and Mary Courtenay must have walked as we are doing now, Jenna thought, wondering if Duke were thinking the same thing.

For a while, they rested beneath the huge vine-twisted oak that sheltered the tree house, their backs against its trunk and Jenna's head on Duke's shoulder. From that vantage point they could look out over the orange grove to the valley below.

Quietly, he talked to her of his boyhood and Ed T., of how he had come to take his place in the family and won respect, of the plans he and his father had discussed for the future, plans he would now carry out alone. With a certain studied gentleness he inquired about her own estimate of her future—what she planned to do with her writing talent, any goals she might have about assuming a place of control in her own family's business.

A bit embarrassed because her thoughts on the matter

were so vague, Jenna confessed she hadn't given it much consideration.

"I guess I didn't look much beyond the next day or the next week," she said. "Like you, I thought my father would always be around."

Later they got up and walked down an avenue of eucalyptus planted by a former owner of the place toward the barns and stables. On that day in that company, wrapped up though she was in him, she found it easy to note small pleasures with sharp awareness: the pattern of a butterfly's wings, gossamer threads of cobwebs.

After they had inspected several saddle horses he kept and talked with Moses Carter, his foreman, Duke suggested a swim.

"There's not much up here for lunch anyway," he said.

In Mary Courtenay's room she changed into her white bikini, then joined him in the hall.

"Beautiful," he remarked, looking her up and down. "But you know you're courting trouble again."

Heated by Duke's caretaker, the water was warm and clear. It dripped and splashed with sunlight as, side by side, they swam lazy lengths. Quietly they persisted in their earlier conversation, their voices—hers soft and his deep—making a counterpoint.

Touching was part of their talk. Jenna realized that, though Duke made no explicit overtures, his touch rested easily on her now, as if an intimacy that went beyond the sexual had been established between them.

Finally she got out to rub herself vigorously with a thick terry towel. Dry and quiet in the sun on the smooth tiles surrounding the pool, she found the day warm enough to get a tan. Eyes narrowed in the strong sunlight, Duke had watched her ascend the ladder before diving underwater to swim several vigorous lengths.

Lying there, she tried not to want him too much. He's still grieving, she thought. What he wants from me now is companionship. But she couldn't help thinking how it would be if he slept with her that night in the high old four-poster, just as she'd imagined the day she had promised to be his girl.

Still in the pool, he came to lean his elbows on the tiles beside her. His wet, slicked-back hair reminded her of how it had been the night her bikini top had floated away. Compellingly, his light, beautiful eyes looked into hers.

"You have a slim, lovely body, Jenna," he said slowly, appraising it before returning his gaze to her own. "Soft and curving in all the right places. But slim. If someday you . . . *loved* someone, the way Mary Courtenay loved my father, would you let him give you a child? Let yourself grow heavy and ungainly with his love?"

The smoldering question hanging there between them, he reached up with one hand to lay it palm down on her stomach.

She was overcome. "I . . . can't imagine any greater joy," she said simply, adding silently and fiercely to herself: Duke Tyrell, don't you know you're that man?

"You're more woman than any I've known," he said softly in that deep voice of his, bringing his mouth down on hers.

His kiss was long and full of passion, an oasis in the dry spell caused by Ed T.'s death. Then he gave her a little squeeze.

"C'mon, get back in the water with me," he said. "I want you near."

About three o'clock, they went up to the house to clean up and change before going into Brooksville for a steak dinner. Jenna went into the bathroom first for a long, languorous shower and shampoo that left her feeling both relaxed and invigorated, full to the brim again with tender longing and remembering.

Duke had opened the long windows that led from the bedroom onto the veranda so that the curtains billowed softly inward. While he took his turn in the bath, she toweled dry, and then stood in lace-trimmed bikini panties before the pier glass to dry her hair, noting the shape of her bare breasts and stomach, thinking of the question he'd asked her.

How would I look, she wondered, if I were carrying his child?

Suddenly, though the door to the hall was shut, she felt his eyes on her. Swiftly she turned to face the veranda windows. He was standing there, bare to the waist in a pair of old cutoffs, still damp from the shower. His face, she saw, betrayed his desire for her.

"Rapunzel," he teased gently, his aquamarine eyes narrow and smoky the way she remembered.

Her lips parting softly, she stood, hairbrush in hand, her hair cascading about her shoulders. "Darling," she breathed, her voice all throaty with wanting him.

"Will you let me make love to you again?" he asked.

But the answer was there already, written all over her face.

11

Wordlessly, Jenna held out her arms. Coming into them, he drew her up tightly against him, so that her breasts were held firmly against the tangled, silky mat that covered his chest. One hand curved around her hip, molding her to intimate knowledge of his desire. The other was caught in her hair, clean and shining, even more golden now from so much sunlight.

Then he was sweeping her up in his arms and carrying her to the bed, lying down with her on the cool sheets. Mary Courtenay's down pillows cushioned her head. Moaning softly, Jenna cradled Duke's dark head against her. His mouth had found her breast to suckle firmly, forging her desire into a white-hot rage of longing.

As before, she felt herself go achingly open within, ready to receive him. I must be crazy, she thought, because I want him to give me the child I was imagining, to sow in me the seeds of his immortality.

He seemed to sense the magnitude of her surrender. With a deep groan, he trailed his kisses from one breast to the other, kneading the first nipple, hard and still damp from his mouth, with his thumb.

She could feel the throbbing outline of his maleness against her leg, offered to her in the way he offered his entire glorious panther self, all the domineering arrogance and unexpected gentleness that he was. Even more than before, she wanted to possess him, to capture somehow the mystery of his maleness and surround it with her own female warmth, while he ravaged her very core.

"Duke," she cried softly, touching him, heedless now of any shyness or learned propriety. "Since that day . . . at your apartment . . . I've needed you so much."

He paused in the midst of nuzzling her breasts with warm blunt little kisses to shoot her a look.

"Do you think I haven't felt it too?" he asked. "Nothing . . ." Firm lips and tongue pulled moistly at one nipple. "*Nothing* could heal the hurt the way this can."

His need overwhelmed her. Rolling partway onto her side, she tugged at the snap closure on the waistband of his shorts.

"I don't need these," he said thickly, covering her hand with his own. "Do I, sweetheart? And you don't need those flimsy little panties."

Keeping one arm around her so that the rhythm of their touching was not broken, he unzipped his shorts and discarded them. Then he was sliding her bikini pants off her hips as she arched away from the bed to help.

Naked, their bodies converged with a sweetness that left her breathless even as something elemental warmed and deepened in her, exerting its power. Yet, as before, he did not rush headlong to consummation. Watching her face as if to fuel his own longing and delight with hers, he drew out the ritual of touch, stroking her breasts and thighs, the backs of her knees, her feet.

Desire stabbed through her, so exquisite it was almost painful, then intensified as his mouth revisited the path his hands had taken. Errant, willful, his kisses kindled her already heated skin, lingering in the little hollows beside her pelvic bones, on the silky skin of her inner thighs. With his tongue he traced the shape of her knees, her ankles, the sensitive, arching soles of her feet, wringing from her little gasps of pleasure.

"Duke, I can't wait anymore," she wailed softly. "Please . . . come inside me. . . ."

In response, he cast her a smoldering look and moved back up to cover her with the length of his body. Clinging to him desperately, she shuddered at the feel of his hard strength. He gave a little groan, his breath hot against her throat.

"You win, darling. We don't have to hold back anymore. I can take you again, be your lover without any qualms, now that the story isn't between us. . . ."

Parting her thighs, he moved into her the way she wanted, entering her with an exquisite thrust of his hard male desire. It sent her senses rocketing even as she arched forward to meet it in her rage to possess him to the utmost.

Full of him, she was half mindless with delight, yet aching for more, more. She felt him tremble at the brink of consummation and then hold back, willing himself to prolong their joy.

"I'm so deep in you," he whispered.

"It's where I want you to be. Since the first night we were together . . . I've always wanted to give you everything."

"I know. I love you so much."

There was no longer any need for words. Heady with what he had told her and moving against his renewed thrusting with enraptured abandon, she was swept to heights of pleasure that surpassed even those they had shared before.

From the moment he had entered her, they had been one person, forged into an intense unity by the heat of their passion, locked in unison as ever-sharper tides of feeling lapped molten around them. Then, when Jenna thought she must burn to ashes with the heat of their love, the exquisite sensations that had been warming and spiraling in her exploded into spasms of pleasure that were like firebursts, lighting up her being.

Carried out of herself, she felt as if her body and mind and spirit had fused, both with the universe and with this man, who was everything to her. A second later, Duke too was out of control, and her pleasure deepened even more as she reveled in the peaking joy that shuddered through his so-loved body.

Gradually, they quieted. If contentment can be so deep that it invades your every cell, then that is what I'm feeling, Jenna thought, her arms loosely around him now.

"I love you so much," he said again.

"And I love you."

He was still beside her when they heard the front door downstairs open and shut. For a moment they lay motionless.

"Mister Duke?" It was Moses Carter's voice. "Are y'all upstairs?"

Duke swore under his breath as the caretaker mounted the first steps with his heavy tread. "Damn," he said, moving apart from her and getting up to pull on his shorts. "Hold tight, darling, I'll have to see what he wants."

Jenna drew the top sheet over herself as he went to open the bedroom door a little and stood blocking any view of the room with his body.

"There you are," said Carter, with a note of relief. "I let the phone ring and ring but y'all didn't hear it." There was an awkward pause. "Mister Neddy's done wrapped his car around a tree and he's in the emergency room at Jackson Memorial."

"Dear God!" Jenna exclaimed softly, not caring now if the old man guessed what they'd been doing in the bedroom together.

"Are you sure about this?" Duke spoke the words with tight control.

"Yessir."

Duke bowed his head a little. "Go back downstairs

160

now, please," he said, "and call Miss Caroline. Tell her we're on our way."

When he turned to face her, there was a look of anguish on his face.

"It was because of Ed T. . . ." Jenna began.

He nodded. "And the way none of us gave him a hand through this thing." His deep voice echoed with remorse. "If anything has happened to him, it'll be partly my fault."

"No," said Jenna, getting up and going to him, putting her arms around him. "You had your own grief and you didn't realize . . ."

But in a way, she knew he was right. They had been thinking only of each other.

"You know, don't you," Duke was saying as he enfolded the still warm, naked length of her, "how much I wanted us to sleep here together tonight, to make love again and again, all night long?"

She nodded, suddenly tremulous. He ran one finger along her cheek and down her neck to just faintly brush the uptilted curve of her breast.

"Can you forgive me for this, sweetheart?"

"There's nothing to forgive." Summoning what will-power she could, she gently pushed him away from her and began to dress. "Of course, we have to go to him."

They were in the car, driving too quickly down the narrow lane toward the estate's iron gate, when she remembered something.

"What did you mean upstairs about the story not being between us now?" she asked.

He gave her a quick glance, his mind already absorbed with the trouble ahead. "Only that with Ed T. gone you wouldn't have any reason to write it, so our unfinished business is settled. We can be to each other what we want."

"Oh." Something had gone cold in her at his words, driving all the lovely intimate feeling away, as she realized that they might be on a collision course, one that could sunder them from each other for good.

He didn't notice her withdrawn manner. Or, if he did, he probably thought she was still harboring frustration at the rude interruption to the loving idyll he'd planned.

"Tell me that I pleased you," he said into the little silence that suddenly lay between them.

"You must know how much you did."

"I always want to do that," he said, putting an arm around her.

"Jenna, will you stay until I can work something out . . . ?"

She was silent a moment. "What excuse will I have, if not the story?" she asked finally.

"There's the small fact that I need you."

Jenna hesitated. I can't tell him now that I intend to go ahead with the story even though Ed T. is gone, she thought. Not with Neddy in danger. But I'll have to, and soon—though I may lose him as a result.

To Jenna's relief, they learned soon after arriving at the hospital that Neddy would be all right. Swathed in bandages, with two bruised and blackened eyes smudging a face that was ashen under his tan, Neddy was still in the small emergency room of Dade City's cottage hospital. He grimaced as a cast was applied to his broken left arm.

"You gave us a hell of a scare," said Duke roughly, grasping his nephew's free hand. "What happened?"

"Whiskey and Valium," said Neddy, in shaken but still ironic tones. "Stupid of me, I know."

Duke gave a rueful shake of his head. Feigning nonchalance, Neddy still held tightly to Duke's hand as the young intern and several nurses bent over him.

"We were awfully worried, you know," Jenna said, feeling a surge of sympathy for this intelligent and quite charming young man who, like his own father, seemed bent on self-destruction.

Neddy turned his brown, purple-ringed eyes on her.

"You must have been," he said, "to come flying over here from Holly Hill the way you did."

Of course, Duke had left word where he would be. That went without saying, now that he was the head of the family. And so their love affair had been no secret from any of the Tyrells.

Jenna met Neddy's gaze steadily, without reply.

"You're damn right we were," said Duke, probably oblivious to the undercurrent of their little exchange. "We can't afford to lose you, kid."

A consultation with the emergency room physician after the cast was completed revealed that Neddy had no head injuries more serious than a slight concussion. He would have to remain in the hospital for a day or two. The young intern added that a charge of reckless driving was pending the patient's release. As Duke told her on the way out, it wouldn't be Neddy's first.

Stopping to examine the wrecked Trans-Am, they drove on to the Bar-T to be with Aunt Bliss and Caroline. Duke and Caroline would return to the hospital that evening during visiting hours.

"Stick by me, sweetheart," Duke told her as he parked the car, repeating his earlier plea. "I'll make it up to you. But I have to be a family man for a few more days."

Jenna nodded and squeezed his hand, preoccupied with her own uneasy thoughts. Somehow she would have to broach the subject of the story to Duke and brave his wrath. Or, worse still, maintain a firm resolve in the face of his gentle, reasonable arguments. But how could she when she loved him so much?

Here, walking across the gravel turnaround drive to the house with her fingers laced through his, that love was as strong as it had been in Mary Courtenay's bed at Holly Hill. Only the flame of desire burned low. But it still burns, thought Jenna, tightening her grasp of his hand. It's ready to flare up again in seconds.

"You're my girl, aren't you?" he asked.

"Yes, darling," she said softly.

"Thank God for that."

Supper that night was a quiet affair. Afterward, when Duke and Caroline left to go back to the hospital and Aunt Bliss murmured something about retiring early, the house seemed unbearably empty.

If Ed T. were here, we'd probably be sitting in his study, storying. He'd be warming up to relish some ribald or amusing tale over a glass of "toothache medicine."

God, how I miss him, she thought. With a sigh, she went up to her room to sort through all the notes and old photos and rolls of film she had amassed for Ed T.'s profile.

I don't trust myself not to turn them over to Duke and just back off now, she realized. The way I feel, I don't know if I can hold out against him.

On impulse, she went back downstairs and borrowed brown wrapping paper, a cardboard box, string, and mailing tape from Mrs. Haskins. Wrapping the old photos carefully in tissue, she packed everything in the box and addressed it to her Uncle Gene at *Second City* magazine. She had called him just after Ed T.'s death to let him know how things stood, so he probably wouldn't be too surprised to receive the package.

At supper she had heard Duke mention something about Wayne going into Dade City in the morning to pick up some legal papers. She would have him post the parcel, and the decision would be out of her hands.

Walking down to Wayne's cottage, she entrusted him with her package and gave him a sum that would be more than sufficient for express postage. Though the foreman raised his brows a bit in curiosity, he acceded to the request without raising any questions and bid her a laconic good night.

With mixed relief and dread, she went back upstairs to the pink and white room that had belonged to Neddy's grandmother. By this time, it felt like home to her, a haven, and she kicked off her shoes to lie down on top of the bed's seersucker spread and turned out the lamp.

She wouldn't undress, so that she could go down to meet Duke on his return. But she was fast asleep and dreaming when finally he did come. She did not hear his soft knock or do more than stir when he pulled a quilt over her.

Jenna woke in the morning quite early. She was alone in the breakfast room with the day's paper and her coffee when she saw Wayne Keeper's jeep take off down the drive in a cloud of gravel dust. That's that, she said to herself shakily, the hot coffee suddenly seeming to burn her throat.

Duke came in five minutes later. At first, she didn't note the set of his jaw, the tight lines around his mouth, didn't see the new and piercing glitter of his aquamarine eyes.

"Hi," she said. "Thank you for putting the quilt over me. At least, I presume you're the one who did."

He nodded.

"How's Neddy?"

"Doing fine." He took a chair. "I have to talk to you, Jenna," he said.

And for the first time, she noticed his deadly serious manner. Suddenly she found herself meeting a proud and stern face, eyes that were as coldly appraising as if she were a witness for the opposition in a lawsuit. Distrust was written on his every feature. Only faintly could she discern the affection she had come to know, the desire to believe in her that was already half-buried under doubt.

"Duke, what is it?" she asked. "What's wrong?"

But in her heart, she knew already. Neddy had told him about the pictures, she thought.

His next words confirmed her supposition. "Neddy says you took a lot of photos at the funeral," he said evenly in what was almost a stranger's voice. "Is that true?"

"Yes."

She felt all sick and cold, her stomach like lead.

"*Why*, Jenna? To make a fool out of me? And plaster

165

my family's grief across the pages of your magazine? Surely not for your memory book!"

The words cut her like a lash. "Which accusation shall I answer first, counsel?" she retorted with more bravery than she really felt.

His eyes narrowed. "I wish you could have been there last night," he said. "Caroline, thank God, was out in the hall, seeing about water for some flowers or something. She admires and likes you. It would have been a terrible disillusionment."

"Leave Caroline out of it." Her voice was now as cold as his own. "This is between us. How have I made a fool out of you?"

"You might have warned me." Not answering directly, he passed a hand over his eyes, as if he hadn't slept. But his anger didn't diminish.

"When Neddy asked if I knew what I was getting into with you, I laughed at him," he said. "'I know,' I told him. 'Oh,' he said. 'So you don't *mind* about the pictures she took at the funeral for her magazine.' He might as well have kicked me in the stomach."

Remorse flooded her. Unerringly he had attacked the one weak spot in her argument, the point on which she could not claim righteousness.

I should have told him, she thought in anguish. Why didn't I have the courage to tell him?

"Duke . . ." she began, stretching out a hand to him.

He rebuffed it. "I want to know something, and I want to know it now," he said. "*Are those pictures for publication?*"

"They might be," Jenna said.

"Damn it, I want a straight answer!" He got to his feet, towering over her.

"I don't expect you to understand this," she said, wishing she could crawl under the table or simply die. "But I plan to write a tribute to Ed T., one that will show the kind of person he was and how much we all loved him. If the pictures I took illustrate that feeling, then yes, I plan to use them."

She got to her feet. A muscle twitched alongside his mouth and he clenched his fists, as if it cost him an effort not to slap her.

"Over my dead body you will," he said in an ominous tone.

"There's nothing you can do about it."

He stared at her. "And to think I fancied myself in love with you," he said. "You're nothing but a cheap sensationalist, a traitor who *used* me—and my father, God rest him—to gain her own ends. Are you planning to do a sidebar on how it feels to make love to Duke Tyrell?"

Jenna's mouth had come open at the spate of name-calling. "If you love me the way you said, how can you say such things?" she asked now. How can you make a cruel joke of what we shared? she added silently to herself.

Duke's voice was hard and cold. *"Loved,"* he said. "Definitely in the past. An up-and-coming writer like you wouldn't want to get her tenses mixed up."

He paused, still so near and yet a million miles from her now. "I'll give you until noon to bring the film from those pictures to me in my office," he said. "After that, you're free to go."

Turning on his heel, he left her.

She sat down again, shaken, the tears running down her cheeks now that he could not see them. He never once tried to see my side of it, she thought, and now I've lost him, the way I knew I would. Even though I'd rather be shot than refuse him anything.

For the space of several minutes, she sat there, her head pillowed on her arms beside her cooling coffee, not thinking rational thoughts but only feeling the ache of his hatred spread until it seemed to be one with her being.

The only sensible thing to do is pack and leave, she thought. Maybe that way I can avoid a scene. But she didn't really have much hope of escaping the Bar-T without another encounter with him.

Back up in her room again, she piled her things into the two suitcases she'd brought. She wasn't sure what personal possessions she'd left behind at Bliss Sanford's house or Duke's own two residences. And she felt light handed without the film and notes.

But thank God I sent them, she whispered to herself, as she started down the stairs with a furtive glance at the closed door of his bedroom. And with that, she realized she had coldly embarked on a course that would maintain her integrity as a writer, even if the woman in her was wounded to the quick.

I owe him an apology, she thought. But that's all.

The door to his study was also closed, probably to discourage visits from other members of the family. He would be sitting there waiting for her, alone in his anger and sorrow and betrayal. Afraid to go past his door down the hall and out the back way, she opted for the front veranda and the gravel turnaround.

Wayne Keeper was just leaving the garage as she entered it a few moments later. He eyed her suitcases.

"I didn't know you were going," he said.

"Only for a week," she lied. "A friend and I are going down to the Keys. Did you post my package?"

"Yes, ma'am. Can I help you with those things?"

"No, please," said Jenna, adding brightly to cover her panic, "They're not heavy, really. Well, see you later."

With shaking hands, she piled the cases into her rental car and started the engine several minutes later. I can't appear to be in a hurry, she thought, backing out at a sedate pace and turning to head up the drive.

Her heart sank when she saw that there were people at the gate. Wayne must have gone directly in to Duke for the two of them were standing at the end of the drive along with several ranch hands. Duke was ordering the gates closed.

She braked as she came up to them and rolled down her window. The door isn't locked, she thought. But I don't dare do that now.

"What do you plan to do?" she asked. "Hold me prisoner? You couldn't give me a more sensational story if you tried."

Duke's fury at the scandal she had created in front of his men was awesome. But it's his fault too, she thought. He can't keep me here.

"I'd appreciate it if you'd open that gate," she said as calmly as she could.

"She's right, Mister Duke," said Wayne painfully in a low voice. "She could press charges if you don't let her go."

"Not until I get those pictures. And the negatives. Or the film, if that's all there is." Implacably, he put out his hand. "Give them to me. You have no right to make a mockery of us."

Jenna winced. "I don't have them," she said.

"You're lying."

She shook her head. "Wayne posted all my pictures and notes to Chicago this morning, from Dade City. Express. The package should be there tomorrow."

Wayne swore softly.

"Is this true?" asked Duke, turning to him.

The foreman took a deep breath. "I don't know for sure, Mister Duke," he said. "But I did post a package for her."

For a moment, Duke closed his eyes. When he opened them, all the light had gone out, leaving them hard and cold. They looked like eyes that would never hold love or trust or appreciation again.

I wonder if it was really true that you loved me, Jenna thought, bereft. But she supposed that was now an academic question.

She felt no surprise when he motioned with a little defeated gesture for one of the men to open the gate.

"Go on," he told her, in a voice for her ears alone. "I hope I never set eyes on you again."

Without answering, she shoved the automatic shift into drive and took off with a spurt of gravel that would have done him credit. Duke, she thought, not even pausing to look back at him as she turned down the highway, I love you with all my heart. And I probably always will.

12

~~~~~~~~~~

As she drove, she tried to plan, ignoring the aching stone of her heart, the thought of that dead, opaque look in Duke's beautiful eyes. I won't call Paul or Rena or go over to the magazine office if I can help it, she decided. I don't trust myself to see them right now.

But she didn't want to stay in an impersonal motel room either. The emptiness there would draw memories of Duke's smile and mouth and thick, springy hair. . . .

Stop it! she told herself in desperation. A motel will be all right. If you're lucky, you'll get a flight out of here tonight, and you'll never even spend much time in the room.

You gave him up for a story, chided her inner voice. A one-of-a-kind man like that. You'll find other people to write about besides Ed T. But never another Duke Tyrell.

Well, what kind of woman would he be getting if I caved in, she answered angrily, her knuckles white on the wheel. Certainly not one with the courage of her convictions. I wouldn't be much better than the kind of person he thinks I am.

Suddenly, as she approached the turnoff for the interstate, she spotted a gas station with a phone booth and thought of Beth Kidder, who would probably be working at her job with the *Tribune* at this very moment. She would go to Beth's to arrange for her flight and wait there until it was time to go to the airport.

Luckily Beth was in. Reporterlike, Jenna's friend asked

a few sharp but impersonal questions, then extended her unadorned sympathy.

"I'll call my landlady and she can give you the key," Beth said. "If you're still there, I'll be home by eight or so and we can talk. If not, good luck."

Jenna's hand rested hesitantly on the receiver after she had hung up. I have to apologize to him, she rationalized. I can't leave Florida without doing that, at least.

With trembling fingers, she dialed the familiar Bar-T number. Caroline answered. "Jenna!" she exclaimed. "What happened? Duke is acting like he's mad enough to kill someone and at the same time as if his heart is broken. Did the two of you have a fight?"

"I . . . can't talk about it, Caroline," she managed. "You'll have to trust me. Just keep believing that I love him, no matter what anybody tells you."

She paused, swallowed, while the line hummed with Caroline's unspoken questions.

"Could I . . . please speak to him?" Jenna added.

"Of course." The response was like a rush of sympathy. "I'll get him for you."

Jenna felt hot and cold and thoroughly, miserably ill there in the roadside phone booth, buffeted by the backlash from semitrailer trucks and her own emotions, while she waited for Duke to come on the line.

"Hello," he said at last, sounding farther away than the five miles or so she had put between them. "What do you want?"

"To . . . to . . . say I'm sorry . . ." she began, and discovered to her horror that she was crying in great ragged gulps that he would be able to hear.

She clapped her hand over the mouthpiece for a moment, struggling to regain control.

"Jenna!" His voice was as stern as she remembered, but with a note of distress in it too. "Where are you? Are you coming back?"

Darling, she thought, I want to, more than anything else in the world.

"I can't," she wailed softly. "Not until I finish the story. I . . . just want to tell you . . . I didn't mean to hurt you, and that you mean everything to me. . . ."

There was a long silence. "I don't believe you," he said finally. "If I mean so much to you, then you wouldn't do this to us."

"I have to," she sobbed. "Don't you . . . love me anymore?"

Again silence hummed on the wire. "No," he said.

With a moan, she replaced the receiver in its cradle. Good-bye, Duke, my darling, she whispered as she stood there. Good-bye. Even if I never get to see you or touch you again, I'm glad I was privileged to know the full ecstasy of your love.

Beth's apartment was plain and quiet, with only stacks of books and a few green plants to perk up the monotony of tired used furniture. It suited Jenna's mood. Her first call to a major airline ticketing office resulted in a reservation for six P.M.

I'm in luck, she thought ironically, taking a can of soda from the refrigerator and curling up on the lumpy sofa to wait. Duke can't find me now, even if he changes his mind.

It was warm in Chicago for February—forty degrees and raining. The next day the rain had turned to damp and fog.

Her weekend, spent alone in her Lake Shore Drive apartment, was painful beyond belief. On Monday, refusing to tell her uncle much about what was causing her wan look and red-rimmed eyes, she had gone to her corner of the editorial room of the magazine offices.

Her hands on the typewriter keys seemed incongruously tan for the damp, bleak day. And the little hollows between my fingers ache, she thought, for the interweaving touch of Duke's handclasp.

Brusquely, she forced herself to concentrate on the business at hand. I won't think of him, she vowed.

173

As always, even when things were going badly in her personal life, the story just came anyway. Almost absent-mindedly, she sat there, letting words pour out by themselves onto the page, her analytical faculty balancing and correcting, while her critical faculty remained dormant. Despite her detachment, she knew the story would be a good one—even great.

With the old photos of the Tyrell family beside her on the desk and proof sheets of the new film she'd shot, she worked there for three lost days, starting early and hunching over her notes far into the evenings, drinking coffee but forgetting to eat, glancing unseeingly at her co-workers as she waited for the next line to come. Somehow, without much prompting from her conscious mind, she was finding the words to weave the pattern of affection and truth and irony and mistakes, of sorrow and joy and fulfillment, that had been Ed T.'s life, to define the essence of what he had been.

This story had to be told, she thought with bitter satisfaction as she finished it, applied the last proofing marks, and gathered up the photos and proof sheets. I was right to go away. But, even as she laid her entire project on her Uncle Gene's desk, a proof sheet fell out, one that showed Duke's haunted-looking face at the funeral, circled by yellow wax crayon, and she felt a stab of guilt and sorrow in her heart.

Once the story was complete, the pain came crowding back. Guessing at her unhappiness, her uncle sent her away from Chicago again, to Springfield and the state legislature. When she returned to her Lake Shore Drive apartment, there was a letter from Duke waiting. She tore it open with cold, awkward fingers.

"Dear Jenna," he had written. "Your uncle sent me an advance copy of the story. It's beautiful—not at all what I'd feared—and we all love it here. You write about my father as if you'd known him all your life. I guess it was true when you said that you loved him.

"Caroline and Aunt Bliss and even Neddy miss you,

but I don't think any of them could long for you the way I do. I was hot-tempered and cruel and arrogant, and I know I hurt you badly. But do you think you could forgive me and let me back into your life?

"I called several times at your office and they told me you had gone to Springfield to watch legislators boondoggle and get into fistfights. When you get back and find this letter in your box, will you call me and tell me I still mean something to you? I've tried, but I can't get your unlisted number.

"Please, Jenna. Forgive and be my girl."

He had signed the little note, "Yours, Duke."

She reread it with her heart in her throat. God, how I longed to hear those words that day in the phone booth beside Interstate 75, she thought. I would have died to hear them then.

Somehow, now, it seemed too late. It wasn't that she loved Duke any the less, she knew. Rather it was that *his* love didn't seem any greater than before. If I were there, within the sight and sound and scent of him, she admitted shakily, I would give in. But now I'm safely out of temptation's way and it's better left like that. I would have wanted to bear his child and be the love of his lifetime. But all he wants is for me to be his "girl."

Once his lover, always in love with him, she thought, sadly classifying herself with Vicki Howard and Mary Lou Davies. He's loved many women before and he will again. The longer we were together, the more difficult this would be. Smoothing the letter with her hand, she put it away in a drawer.

Somehow the letter seemed to mark the end of her relationship with Duke rather than a new beginning. During the next week, she acceded to Bob Czerny's pleas and began again to accompany him to plays and concerts and dinners in their favorite ethnic Chicago restaurants. He wasn't Duke, but then no one could be. In his own way, Bob was a good companion with a quiet, understated sense of humor that soothed her frazzled nerves.

Yet she missed Duke keenly at odd moments, like a Saturday morning when she was washing her hair and thinking of how they'd been together, that last time, at Holly Hill. Or at a matinee performance of the Chicago Symphony one cold Sunday in mid-March. A guest violinist with the symphony played a piece by Schubert that reminded her of their Guarnieri evening, with all its champagne, the heady kisses, and then the incongruous night spent as lovers who hadn't made love.

The longing she'd felt that night had been healed later, when they'd slept together at his apartment after the freeze. But the rapture had turned to ashes, as cold as the Chicago winter, leaving only the ache of unfulfilled desire in its place. Without being able to stop herself, she thought of the letter that had gone unanswered and how Duke must have given up waiting by now for a reply. I should have gone to him, she thought. Why didn't I? And she answered herself: I was a fool.

Unconsciously, she sighed, her eyes misting over with tears.

Bob Czerny patted her hand. "It's still that Tyrell fellow in Florida, isn't it?" he said.

Outside Orchestra Hall, the snow that had been predicted earlier had finally arrived. It was falling in big, wet, starry flakes to hush the traffic sounds and blur the shapes of the Art Institute lions across Michigan Avenue.

Softly it settled on the black limousine, shiny as a grand piano, that had pulled up to the curb, and on the row of taxis behind it. As she watched, the limousine door opened.

Incredibly, *he* stepped out, in a heavy overcoat with a dark fur collar, as tall and beautiful as ever, still a man in a million. His dark head was bare to the wind, his hair furring with snowflakes.

"Duke!" she exclaimed.

He simply stood there, waiting, and she cast an anguished glance at Czerny.

"Go on, Jenna," said her friend, squinting approval at her from behind his spectacles. "For once you know what you want."

She needed no further urging. Like one released from bondage or a bad dream, she ran to him, and was lifted off her feet to be enfolded in his arms.

"Ah, sweetheart," he said, his breath smoking in the cold. "You have snowflakes on your lashes." And then he added, "Let's get in the car."

She gave herself over to him. With a little salute to Czerny, he settled her inside and took her again in his arms.

"Miller's Pub," he told the chauffeur, and brought his mouth down on hers.

They had no need at all for words. For Jenna, Duke's mouth and the feel of him again in her arms was enough. Eagerly she returned his caresses, kissing his cheek, delicious with scented after-shave and ruddy with cold, his mouth, the warmth of his neck.

What did it matter that she could never keep him, if she could have him for a while? She had been dying of her need for him.

Slowly their limousine moved through the city lights and curiously muffled traffic as they went deeper into each other's embrace. At last, they pulled to the curb in front of the restaurant Duke had named, a favorite of Jenna's. It was warmed by stained glass and oil paintings and had always seemed like a haven on wet or wintery nights.

"What are you doing here?" she asked finally as he drew back to look at her. "How did you find me?"

His aquamarine eyes narrowed and he regarded her from beneath straight, dark lashes. "I came looking for you. Your Uncle Gene told me where."

As usual, the power of his personality seemed to overcome her inhibitions. "I've missed you so much," she confessed. "I'm . . . wild about you, you know."

"*Are* you?" Still looking at her with that intense gaze, he raised one brow at her in the way she loved. "Well, how do you suppose *I* feel?"

"I . . . couldn't guess."

Suddenly she felt precariously poised on the brink of the most important discovery of her life.

"I lied to you that day on the phone," he said. "I love you more than life and I want to marry you. But first of all, I want to take you back to Holly Hill tonight. Let's go inside and have a bite to eat while we talk it over."

His words, spoken in that deep, soft, accented voice she had heard even in her dreams, caught her by surprise. Somehow she managed to do as he suggested, to allow the chauffeur to help her out of the car and to enter the pub on Duke's arm.

This can't be real, she thought, as they checked their coats and followed the hostess between rows of cozy tables, through the cheerful low din of knives and forks and conversation, to a booth in the corner.

True to form, Duke ordered without even glancing at the menu.

"That was a beautiful story you wrote," he said, turning to her and taking her hands in his as the waitress hurried away. "It made me cry, something I haven't done since that night in the boathouse. Why didn't you answer my letter?"

"I . . . didn't dare."

He gave her a look. "I thought maybe you were still mad at me," he said, "for the stupid way I'd behaved. Or that you were glad to wash your hands of the crazy lot of us and be back in your big-city routine."

Duke paused. "You see, I took it for granted that you knew I loved you, despite the awful things I'd said. But I also knew you weren't the sort of girl to have a casual affair. So the natural conclusion was that you didn't want to give up your Chicago job to be a rancher's wife."

Jenna shook her head. "Duke Tyrell," she said softly. "You can be *such* a fool."

He grinned at her. "That's my girl."

"Yes," she said. "Always that. Why didn't you tell me, that time at Holly Hill, how you felt—that you wanted our love to be permanent?"

"For one thing, I hardly had time. And, as I told you, I wasn't sure what you wanted. I thought if I got you back into bed and made you love me as much as I loved you, you'd *have* to marry me."

"Spoken like a Tyrell. What prompted you to come up here finally?"

"I got tired of life without Jenna Martin."

She smiled at him. "You wouldn't have had to marry me, you know. All you needed to do was crook your little finger and I'd have come running."

"Sorry." His grin was positively wicked now. "It's marriage or nothing with me."

A wave of shyness swept over her. "You've been a confirmed bachelor for years, the despair of the best-looking women you know," she whispered. "Why me?"

His eyes gleamed at her left-handed compliment. "Don't you know, sweetheart? Don't you realize that you're that rare and mystical combination, someone I want to ravish *and* protect?"

Unshed tears glittered in her eyes as she sat there speechless, her hands still held tightly in his, recalling what Aunt Bliss had said about Ed T. and Mary Courtenay. Oh, she thought, I must be the luckiest girl in the world.

"Well?" His mouth was so tender looking she longed to raise her own to it. "Don't keep me dangling. Are you going to marry me and come back to Florida with me tonight?"

Of course, it would have all been arranged already. He would be her lover and husband, and—from now on—the task of falling in with such high-handed last-minute maneuvers would be part of her life.

"You know the answer to that."

"I want to hear you say it. Say *yes.*"

"Yes to anything you want, my darling Duke Tyrell. Yes, I'll marry you."

He kissed her then, creating a slight hush near their table as the other diners paused to look at them with surprise and interest.

"I have something for you," he said at last, producing a small jeweler's box from his pocket.

Jenna was overcome as he snapped it open. Set off against black velvet was the most exquisite ring she'd ever seen: a huge, square-cut aquamarine mounted in white gold and flanked by tiny diamonds.

"Duke!" she exclaimed. "It's absolutely lovely!"

"Getting the aquamarine was Caroline's idea," he admitted. "I can't take credit for it. She said you were crazy about my eyes and this would always make you think of them."

"Caroline was right." Unmindful now that they had an audience, she reached up to kiss him again.

A moment later, he was slipping the ring on her finger.

"There's a wedding band to match," he told her as their food arrived. "Don't dally with your supper. You have a lot of packing to do."

She was still lost in amazement as they drew up in front of her Lake Shore Drive apartment building. It was beyond belief that Duke Tyrell was here in Chicago, walking close beside her, stamping snow off his feet and taking possession of her arm. It was nothing short of a miracle that he loved her and would be her husband.

Then she caught sight of the doorman's face and giggled. "That's one I've *never* pulled on him before," she confided as they got into the elevator. "Going out with one man and coming back with another."

"I should hope not." He flashed her that wicked smile.

Upstairs, she unlocked the door to reveal the parquet floors and Oriental rugs, splashy modern art, and eclectic furniture her mother had chosen. With only the foyer lamp lit, she pulled back the draperies that covered a bank of windows to reveal the lights of Lake Shore Drive below, blurring into haloes in the snowfall.

Then she tossed her sable jacket over a deep, oyster-beige couch and turned to him.

Removing his topcoat, he threw it down beside the jacket. "Where's your bedroom?" he asked.

Her eyes widened a little. "This way," she said.

Trim and graceful in his brown sweater and trousers despite his height and broad shoulders, he followed her into her flowery Queen Anne boudoir. Standing in the midst of its feminine ambience, he was the quintessential male.

"Such a girlish room," he murmured, his mouth warm at the base of her neck as he pulled down the zipper of her short black crepe tunic with one expert hand.

She shut her eyes and leaned back against him, remembering now with her body as well as with her mind just how it had been before with the two of them. As if they had not been apart, she quickened at his touch, felt him do the same. Anticipation, fueled by their knowledge of each other, was like a live current between them.

"It's like Cleopatra's tent, or Helen's couch," she said, "with you here."

For once, she was wearing a bra. Ably, he unhooked it as he bent to kiss a pathway of fire down the length of her backbone. Pleasure shot through her in little waves as he simultaneously unzipped her outfit's matching trousers.

"I'll help you change," he offered belatedly, his muffled humor dissolving into passion as he slid her loosened garments to the floor.

Oh, she thought, to have his hands on me again. . . .

Peeling down her nylons and stepping out of them, she turned to face him, clad only in her silk-and-lace panties, the way she'd been that day at Holly Hill when he had watched her from the veranda window.

"God, but you're beautiful, Jenna," he whispered, urging her backward to the bed. "Even here, in this icy, forsaken winter, your skin has that apricot glow. Your breasts are like satin, your nipples velvet . . ."

But his hands were on her, and her nipples had hardened under them to little nuggets of desire.

"Duke," she moaned, drawing his head down so that his mouth closed over one breast's peak.

Firm, demanding lips tugged at her, touching off almost unbearable ripples of longing. Within her, the haven that would always be his now flooded with pleasure. She shuddered deeply, suddenly, as his strong white teeth just grazed the sensitive skin of her breast.

I want him to take and take and take, she thought, as he bit at her other nipple so gently that the gesture was an ardent caress. With him I am endless. I could go on giving to him forever.

On fire with that deep need to give, she burned out of control in his arms.

I can't wait any longer, she thought desperately, her need for a consummation of their love pushing all else aside. There has been too much waiting between us.

"Duke," she pleaded, clutching at him, "your sweater. For God's sake, take off your things. . . ."

In response, his mouth moved up to brush hers while his thumbs continued to plunder the softness of her breasts.

"*You* take them off me," he said.

His words only deepened her longing. With trembling fingers, she pushed up his sweater to reveal dark chest hair, the broad, rippling muscles her curving palms remembered so well.

Knowing he was hers now, she let her touch linger, stroking her fingers across his chest, kissing his mouth when he completed pulling the sweater over his head. Before this night is through, she thought, I'm going to kiss him everywhere—those flat male nipples that harden like mine with wanting, the taut midsection below his ribs . . .

"Now my trousers, darling," he was saying, his voice

rough with arousal. "I suppose I ought to warn you—I'm not wearing anything underneath."

Awkward from the need that was flowering hotly within her, she did as he asked, her hands brushing against his naked thighs in the process.

"Jenna," he groaned. "Do you know what it does when you touch me like that?"

Then he was taking off her bikini pants and coming into her again, to rock her in the motions of love, drawing her with him up the sweet and fiery path to fulfillment that he'd etched so indelibly on her soul.

How long they wrestled lovingly there together in her tangled bedsheets, hoarsely whispered words of love the only sounds breaking the silence, Jenna couldn't have said. The ascent, as they craved more and more of each other, seemed to go on forever.

Inevitably though, gloriously, they reached the abandoned quivering apex of their communion, with its cataclysmic waves of pleasure, and then drifted slowly afterward into peace and a tingling contentment.

Complete once more, she curled against him, giving herself over to the deep comfort of his embrace, secure in the knowledge that his love would always be there to catch her as she descended from the heights.

"I can't let you sleep, darling," he said apologetically some minutes later. "Moses Carter may not be pounding down our door, but we have a plane to catch."

Yawning, she stretched against him and then cuddled back profoundly into his arms. "Why can't we just stay here tonight?" she said. "There'll be another plane in the morning."

"Right now," he acknowledged, "all I want to do is drift off to sleep with you and then wake up right here to make love again. But our life together will be more than this moment, Jenna."

She lifted her face so that their eyes met and held.

Softly, he continued. "I'm going to spend the rest of

my days pouring a lifetime of love into you so that you never want for anything again. . . ."

She was moved to tears. "But, I don't see . . ." she began.

"I don't want to start here. Maybe that makes me a romantic, but I want our first night back together to be spent at Holly Hill, in Mary Courtenay's bed."

"Oh, Duke. . . ."

"In the morning," he added sweetly, "when you kiss me awake to ask for more of what pleases us best, your hair will come down like a waterfall in the sunlight around her pillow. That bed has been empty of love and pleasure too long."

The tears were stinging her eyes hotly now, spilling over. What a beautiful man he is, she thought again—so full of feeling and real gentleness. All my life I'll want him, more each time we make love. We'll be more and more a part of each other.

"You and your Southern tradition, your ancestor worship," she said, teasing him fondly to get a rein on her emotions. "I love you so much. I . . . suppose I'd better get dressed."

With a brief, hard embrace, he pushed her from him.

"*Yes,*" he said firmly, his eyes raking over her skin as if he half regretted his decision to go. "And *I'd* better not help."

After dressing quickly, he smoothed down the sheets and powder blue spread, then stretched out on the bed to watch her, looking even more devastatingly masculine than ever.

For the trip she chose black wool slacks, a white silk satin open-necked blouse, her mother's pearls. Because it would be cold on the way to the airport, she would wear the sable jacket, too. It would have to go into cold storage at her destination.

When she was ready, he snapped her cases shut. "You can call your uncle and aunt tomorrow," he said, "to invite them to the wedding, after we decide when it's to be."

She nodded.

"You might tell your uncle that you can uphold your end of the family business from Florida, if that'll ease his mind."

She smiled, not wanting him to feel any uneasiness about her career. "I'd already thought of that," she said. "I can write anywhere and I hope someday to get involved with the editorial side of *Bayside*."

"Good. I want you to be happy with me."

Tampa was balmy and clear, the airport with its copper pelicans familiar now, Duke's Mercedes parked in almost the same place it had been the last time they had walked out to it together.

In the car, as they sped north toward Brooksville, she slept again, her head on his shoulder, dreaming fitful but happy dreams. At last, they were turning up the long, narrow drive at Holly Hill and he woke her gently.

"We're home, sweetheart," he said.

She sat up, still in the circle of his arm. Ahead, the huge old house gleamed faintly through tangled oak and bamboo and bougainvillea. There were puddles of moonlight on the grass, milky between the shadows cast by shifting, luminous clouds.

Parking the car in front of the veranda, he helped her out and drew her up the steps. His arm was around her as he fitted his old-fashioned key into the lock.

Then he carried her inside and up the stairs to the door of Mary Courtenay's room. He pushed it open with his foot, to reveal the high old four-poster they'd traveled so far to reach. The pier glass gave back their shadowy reflection.

Sighing, he bent his head. His mouth covered hers, hinting already at the passion she knew would flare between them.

"From this moment on, I consider you my wife, Jenna Martin Tyrell," he said in that fierce way he had when he was feeling something very keenly.

Then, with great tenderness and the leisure of a man who finally has the woman he wants, he put her down on the bed in the moonlight and began slowly to unfasten her clothes.

Silhouette Desire
15-Day Trial Offer
A new romance series
that explores
contemporary relationships
in exciting detail

Four Silhouette Desire romances, free for 15 days!
We'll send you four new Silhouette Desire romances
to look over for 15 days, absolutely free! If you decide
not to keep the books, return them and owe nothing.

Four books a month, free home delivery. If you like
Silhouette Desire romances as much as we think you
will, keep them and return your payment with the
invoice. Then we will send you four new books every
month to preview, just as soon as they are published.
You pay only for the books you decide to keep, and
you never pay postage and handling.

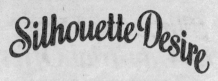

Silhouette Desire

Coming Next Month

Not Even For Love by Erin St. Claire

When a misunderstanding threatened to drive them apart, the memory of their passion drove Jordan to convince Reeves of the truth. His misty green eyes and sensual mouth had lifted her to peaks of ecstasy she could never forget.

Make No Promises by Sherry Dee

Even though Cassie was engaged to another man, she was instantly attracted to Steele Malone. He waged a passionate war on her senses, defying her emotions and lulling her body with primitive pleasures.

Moment In Time by Suzanne Simms

She knew Tyler expected a man to build his treasured dam, but Carly was a fully qualified civil engineer. What began as a battle of wills blazed anew in the Santa Fe sunset, a flashfire passion which consumed them both.

Whenever I Love You by Alana Smith

Diana Nolan was Treneau Cosmetics' new goddess of beauty. Paul Treneau was the boss who whisked her away to his Hawaiian paradise for "business." But she had ignited in him a spark of desire fated to burn out of control.

Get 6 new Silhouette Special Editions every month.

One book always <u>free</u>!

Free Home Delivery, Free Previews, Free Bonus Books.
Silhouette Special Editions are a new kind of romance novel. These are big, powerful stories that will capture your imagination. They're longer, with fully developed characters and intricate plots that will hold you spellbound from the first page to the very last.

Each month we will send you six exciting *new* Silhouette Special Editions, just as soon as they are published. If you enjoy them as much as we think you will, pay the invoice enclosed with your shipment. **They're delivered right to your door with never a charge for postage or handling, and there's no obligation to buy anything at any time.** To start receiving Silhouette Special Editions regularly, mail the coupon below today.

Silhouette Special Editions

Silhouette Special Editions®, Dept. SESD7E
120 Brighton Road, Clifton, NJ 07012

Please send me 6 Silhouette Special Editions, absolutely free, to look over for 15 days. If not delighted, I will return only 5 and owe nothing. **One book is mine free.**

NAME_____

ADDRESS_____

CITY_____

STATE_____ ZIP_____

SIGNATURE_____
(If under 18, parent or guardian must sign.)
This Offer Expires January 31, 1983.

YOU'LL BE SWEPT AWAY
WITH SILHOUETTE DESIRE

$1.75 each

1 ☐ CORPORATE AFFAIR
Stephanie James

2 ☐ LOVE'S SILVER WEB
Nicole Monet

3 ☐ WISE FOLLY
Rita Clay

4 ☐ KISS AND TELL
Suzanne Carey

5 ☐ WHEN LAST WE LOVED
Judith Baker

6 ☐ A FRENCHMAN'S KISS
Kathryn Mallroy

SILHOUETTE DESIRE, Department SD/6
1230 Avenue of the Americas
New York, NY 10020

Please send me the books I have checked above. I am enclosing $_____
(please add 50¢ to cover postage and handling. NYS and NYC residents
please add appropriate sales tax). Send check or money order—no cash or
C.O.D.'s please. Allow six weeks for delivery.

NAME _____

ADDRESS _____

CITY _____ STATE/ZIP _____

Silhouette Desire

Now Available

Corporate Affair by Stephanie James

Kalinda had come to Colorado determined to
avenge a lost love. But she was shaken by
Rand Alastair who conquered and
claimed her wounded heart.

Love's Silver Web by Nicole Monet

When Jace's lips, hot and passionate, came down
on hers, Laura was overwhelmed with desire.
It was just a matter of time before he
possessed her, body and soul.

Wise Folly by Rita Clay

Seven years had not dimmed Diana's desire for
Noah. How could she deny him now, when he
gave her everything she ever longed for
and more?

Kiss And Tell by Suzanne Carey

Jenna tried to free her mind of Duke Tyrell. But
one moonlit night haunted her, when Duke
had captured her heart and mesmerized
her senses with love.

When Last We Loved by Judith Baker

Even the glitter and flash of Nashville's country
music world couldn't compete with the dizzying
rapture Cassie felt in Hoyt Temple's arms.

A Frenchman's Kiss by Kathryn Mallory

In the dark, ripe fields of grapes that stretched
out around them, Jean Paxton abandoned
herself to the searing kisses of a Frenchman
who made her forget . . .

Dear Reader:

Please take a few moments to fill out this questionnaire. It will help us give you more of the Desires you'd like best.

Mail to: **Karen Solem**
Silhouette Books
1230 Ave. of the Americas, New York, N.Y. 10020

1. How did you obtain **KISS AND TELL?**

10-1 ☐ **Bookstore**   -6 ☐ **Newsstand**
 -2 ☐ **Supermarket**   -7 ☐ **Airport**
 -3 ☐ **Variety/discount store**   -8 ☐ **Book Club**
 -4 ☐ **Department store**   -9 ☐ **From a friend**
 -5 ☐ **Drug store**   -0 ☐ **Other:** _____
                                      (write in)

2. How many Silhouette Desires have you read including this one? (circle one number) 11- **1 2 3 4 5 6**

3. Overall how would you rate this book?

12-1 ☐ **Excellent** -2 ☐ **Very good**
 -3 ☐ **Good** -4 ☐ **Fair** -5 ☐ **Poor**

4. Which elements did you like best about this book?

13-1 ☐ **Heroine** -2 ☐ **Hero** -3 ☐ **Setting** -4 ☐ **Story line**
 -5 ☐ **Love scenes** -6 ☐ **Ending** -7 ☐ **Other Characters**

5. Do you prefer love scenes that are

14-1 ☐ **Less explicit than**   -2 ☐ **More explicit than**
       in this book   **in this book**
          -3 ☐ **About as explicit as in this book**

6. What influenced you most in deciding to buy this book?

15-1 ☐ **Cover** -2 ☐ **Title** -3 ☐ **Back cover copy**
 -4 ☐ **Recommendations** -5 ☐ **You buy all Silhouette Books**

7. How likely would you be to purchase other Silhouette Desires in the future?

16-1 ☐ **Extremely likely**   -3 ☐ **Not very likely**
 -2 ☐ **Somewhat likely**   -4 ☐ **Not at all likely**

8. Have you been reading...

17-1 ☐ **Only Silhouette Romances**
 -2 ☐ **Mostly Silhouette Romances**
 -3 ☐ **Mostly one other romance** _____
                                      (write one in)
 -4 ☐ **No one series of romance in particular**

9. Please check the box next to your age group.

18-1 ☐ **Under 18**   -3 ☐ **25-34**   -5 ☐ **50-54**
 -2 ☐ **18-24**   -4 ☐ **35-49**   -6 ☐ **55 +**

10. Would you be interested in receiving a romance newsletter? If so please fill in your name and address.

Name _____

Address _____

City _____ State _____ Zip _____

          19   20   21   22   23